Blazing Paddles

Historical Fiction of British Columbia

Written by the B.C. History Club at
Highland Secondary School

Published by Fuent Productions

FUENT

Canadian Cataloguing in Publication Data

Authors: B.C. History Club at Highland Secondary School
Editor: Gerald W. Fussell
Title: Blazing Paddles: Historical Fiction of British Columbia

Includes some text in French
ISBN 0-9685412-1-6

1. British Columbia – History – Fiction. 2. Historical fiction, Canadian (English) – British Columbia — Comox 3. High school students' writings, Canadian (English) — British Columbia – Comox. 4. Short stories, Canadian (English) – British Columbia – Comox. 5. Canadian fiction – 20th century. 6. Highland Secondary School (Comox, B.C.) I. Highland Secondary School (Comox, B.C.). B.C. History Club.

PS8329.5.B75B43 2000 C813'.081'0832711
C99-901575-3 PR9198.2.B72B43 2000

FUENT PRODUCTIONS
750 Pritchard Avenue, Comox, B.C., V9M 3S8.
Telephone (250) 339-5525 Facsimile (250) 339-0832

PRINTED AND BOUND IN CANADA BY ABC PRINTING OF COURTENAY, B.C.

ISBN 0-9685412-1-6

Artistic Co-ordinator: Nathan Senner
Project Co-ordinator: Gerald W. Fussell

This book is dedicated to all of those who inspire others. It is dedicated to my son Jacob who inspires those who watch him with his pint-sized, indomitable determination and insatiable curiosity. It is dedicated to my wife Stacey, whose strength and faith daily inspire me to push myself. And, it is dedicated to our unborn child who inspires dreaming with its potential which is limitless. Most of all, it is dedicated to those people who dare to dream and who have the courage to pursue their dreams.

Gerald W. Fussell
Project Co-ordinator

Table of Contents

Acknowledgements

A book of this scope and magnitude could not be produced without considerable support and although the students produced this book, they received support from many quarters. Matt Hughes, Jeanette Taylor, Nelson McInnis, and Des Kennedy all donated their time and expertise to work with the writers. These accomplished authors spoke with the students, answered their questions, provided information and helped provide technical support for the writing of this book. Zoe Landale worked with the students doing editorial work and served as a resource for them. Research needs were supported by Bill Barlee, Michael Kennedy, Kathryn Bridge and the staff at the BC Archives.

Without the generous financial support of the Comox Rotary Club, the printing of this book would not have been possible. Similarly, without the unwavering support and encouragement of school administrators Wayne Friesen and Tom Demeo, we would have been unable to present the book you now hold. Numerous teachers also played important supporting roles. George Biggs, Donna Grinnel, Kari Provencher and Josie Andrew helped with the writing of the book while Tracy Richards assisted students with the test layout and the book's webpage. Jeanine Maars and the work experience office helped provide support and credit for much of the book's production. Sophie Boisvert, Dave Brooker, Philippe Brulot, Faith Edwards, Elizabeth Fussell, Roy Fussell, Jaques Gobeil, Shawn Holland, Harlene Holm, Dave Laird, Ron Olson, Lyneita Swanson, and Karen Thatchuk provided editorial assistance.

Nathan Senner created the cover for the book using a collection of ideas from students and was responsible for supporting the artists presented in the book. Roger Rajotte supported the researchers in their efforts to hunt for the pertinent information and details. Brian Mather co-ordinated efforts to prepare a promotional video of the production of *Blazing Paddles*. Jason Gilbert, Margaret Lord, Len Morrow and Bob Thompson have assisted greatly with the marketing.

Without the support of these people and many others whose contributions go unsung, we would not enjoy the success we do. The skills, attitudes, and concepts these people have passed on to the students who have contributed to this project will last a lifetime and will have an impact far beyond the immediate book and students.

Preface

Ezra Pound wrote "It is only after long experience that most men are able to define a thing in terms of its own genus, painting as painting, writing as writing. You can spot the bad critic when he starts by discussing the poet and not the poem" (A, B, C of Reading, 1934, page 71). The stories in this book must stand alone in order to have a fair reading. Each story offers something entirely different for the reader and I would be surprised if any one reader likes all of the stories; I would be equally surprised if any reader enjoys none of the stories. These stories stretch the gamut from pre-human history to the recent arrival of Chinese migrants to our coast. They deal with fact and myth, emotion and action, theme and image. Two of the stories were written in French, one story was written in dialect, and the others have qualities that are equally unique. Suffice it to say this book contains a plethora of stories designed to entertain while accurately depicting the zeitgeist – spirit or essence of an era.

The goals at the beginning of this project were: to produce entertaining history of British Columbia, to produce a book that is profitable in the main-stream market, to produce a collection of critically acclaimed short stories, and to develop personal skills. Each of these goals has been achieved and for that the 200 + students involved should be commended.

Historical Fiction in its broadest sense is the telling of stories set in historically accurate settings. One of the key problems faced by historians and consumers alike is the accessibility of the history. Few people enjoy reading expository diatribes about past events; few historians enjoy reading popular-ised, sensationalised accounts of the past. Good historical fiction is the mar-riage of these two extremes. Noted international author Matt Hughes states that "All too often, historical accuracy takes a pummelling, and the characters are just late twentieth century westerners, with all the preconceptions of our place and time, but stuffed into togas… The other peril for historical fictioneers is to let the history get in the way of the story" (From out of the Past…, 1999). This book avoids either extreme when viewed in its entirety; however, I have little doubt that purists on either side will find individual stories that contra-vene their views of historical fiction. Great pains have been taken to set the stories accurately and to have the events realistic and believable. The model used was that of the late James Michener whose characters and plots were completely fictitious but whose settings and concepts accurately portrayed the zeitgeist.

You have been invited to enter a world through which you can access the past in the comfort of your home. Each story will offer you the opportunity to travel back in time and to take a glimpse at life through the eyes of common, legitimate people. True literature transcends the annals of time and accomplished writers take time to perfect their art. This book contains initial work by several writers who will be heard from in the future and contains stories that will have an impact on people's impressions of our past. You stand at the precipice of unconstrained potential. Enjoy!

Gerald W. Fussell
Project Co-ordinator

Introduction

I can think of no better training for an ambitious young writer than to become involved in a book such as this. It fills a desperate need: as far as I know it is the only work of its kind that trains young students not only in the skills of writing, but also in the various crafts involved in the writing, publishing and editing process, not to mention sales.

A good deal of time is spent in the schools teaching about writing and about history. But in this book the students are treated as professionals: they learn on the job. As I well know, the best way to study history is to learn to write about it; that includes all the techniques of scholarly research combined with the equally necessary skills of popularization.

The young authors who have contributed to this book have been allowed to use their imagination within the disciplines of historical accuracy. Thus, in producing this book they have taken several courses all at once; in writing style, narrative techniques, dialogue, characterization, and plot development. In addition, they have learned to master the hard legwork involved in finding out the details of a colourful but often obscure past.

They are fortunate to be living in one of the most interesting corners of this scattered country. Thus, I doubt if they and those who follow will ever run out of subject matter.

Pierre Berton

Le reflux du moment

Devon Buss

L'aube. Le monde se lève; les créatures secouent la pluie matinale de leurs dos. Les nuages gris-blancs pendent du plafond terrestre. D'en arrière brille le soleil argenté.

Frère Arbre inspire profondément l'odeur de la pluie qui tombe doucement à travers ses branches. De ses racines épaisses, il boit le lait de la terre, frais et clair comme la lumière du matin. Il sourit aux animaux en bas. Un petit faon se déplace sur ses jambes grêles, grignotant les herbes vertes autour du grand tronc.

Frère Arbre s'étend jusqu'à lui et le chatouille tendrement.

«Où est ta mère, petit? Il vaut mieux que tu restes proche d'elle car les étrangers arriveront aujourd'hui.»

Frère Arbre est bon et sage. Il est un brave protecteur des créatures les plus fragiles et un enseignant sensé qui encourage tous les animaux à vivre paisiblement dans la forêt. Depuis plusieurs jours, Frère Arbre surveille la progression lente des étrangers. Il a vu s'approcher les nuages de fumée envoyés dans le ciel au crépuscule. Frère Arbre a vu se lever et se coucher le soleil maintes fois et connaît toutes les créatures de la région, mais ces étrangers posent un mystère. Il a l'intention de les accueillir chaleureusement. Ses intentions envers eux sont bienveillantes. Ils savent apprivoiser le feu, ils doivent être sages.

«Il ne faut pas t'inquiéter, petit. Je crois que les créatures étranges sont nos frères qui ont voyagé depuis des générations. Ils seront fatigués en arrivant. On doit bien les recevoir quand ils arriveront. Ils pourront nous raconter leurs voyages dans des mondes lointains.»

Le petit faon clignote ses gros yeux bruns en direction de la forêt et regarde attentivement Frère Arbre. Trop jeune pour comprendre, le faon file maladroitement et Frère Arbre soupire profondément.

De loin en haut vient soudainement l'appel aïgu d'une mère inquiète.

«Salut, Soeur Orfraie! Où vas-tu, et qu'est-ce qui te tracasse?»

Le corps de Soeur Orfraie est presque camouflé par le ciel gris-blanc, qui descend lourdement sur la tête du grand arbre. Les ailes fortes de l'orfraie la transportent rapidement et facilement à travers les cieux épais. Elle raconte:

«Je viens de voir des créatures très étranges qui s'approchent du Nord. Ils emportent avec eux la flamme domestiquée et ils font des bruits bizarres. Ils ne ressemblent à aucun de nos cousins des bois, des airs, ni des eaux. Ils voyagent sur terre et je ne sais s'ils peuvent voler. Il faut que je me dépêche, pour défendre mon nid.»

Soeur Orfraie ne veut pas rester pour parler avec Frère Arbre, qui lui demande de se percher sur une branche et de se reposer un instant. Pourtant, elle se tient proche de lui, un peu mal à l'aise. La pluie tombe plus copieusement, en éclaboussant de petites gouttes les yeux de Soeur Orfraie. L'arbre lui dit:

«Soeur Orfraie, il ne faut pas t'inquiéter de ces étrangers. Ils sont sages avec leur connaissance du feu et ils voyagent depuis des générations. Ils peuvent nous raconter de merveilleux contes. Peut-être qu'ils savent remédier aux maladies de nos frères mammifères, ou donner le souffle aux bébés qui ne respirent pas à la naissance.

-Mon frère sage, je comprends que vous vouliez qu'ils soient nos frères. Mais, comme on ne sait rien d'eux, ce serait mieux de nous mettre en sécurité plutôt que de risquer nos vies, ou la perte des jeunes aux mains d'un prédateur.

-Ma soeur, ce n'est pas du tout comme ça... »

Frère Arbre attend un instant, en essayant de trouver des mots pour s'exprimer et Soeur Orfraie l'interrompt:

«Je m'excuse, mon frère. J'espère autant que vous que ces étrangers seront nos frères. Mais en attendant, je retourne au nid. Leur arrivée est imminente. Le battement de leurs coeurs remplit l'air. À bientôt, mon frère.

-Oui, je comprends, ma soeur. À bientôt.»

Frère Arbre suit Soeur Orfraie des yeux, jusqu'à ce qu'elle quitte sa vue en passant par-dessus les arbres.

Elle avait raison. La cadence des battements de coeur résonne dans la forêt. Il sait que ces sons ne sont que les salutations des nouveaux arrivants. Soudain, il voit de l'autre côté des bois, les silhouettes des étrangers à poil brun et gris. D'en bas, il entend un froissement dans le feuillage.

«Qui est là?, demande le grand arbre à la bête cachée dans l'arbuste. N'aie pas peur, je ne te ferai pas de mal.

-Ce n'est pas de vous que j'ai peur, vient une réponse entre les froissements de feuilles. La cadence commence à s'accélérer et Frère Arbre ressent les vibrations au fond de ses racines les plus étendues. Je m'inquiète pour les bêtes paisibles de la forêt qui ne peuvent rien faire pour se défendre.

-Se défendre de quoi? Tu ne parles certainement pas des étrangers. Ils sont nos frères. Sors de là, pour que je voie ton visage.»

D'en dessous des buissons sort un petit animal féroce. Ses yeux sont remplis de méchanceté et d'intrépidité, mais le petit corps de Frère Belette frissonne, évidement terrifié et gelé du nez à la queue. La pluie glaciale attaque l'animal à travers son pelage.

«Il faut que toutes les créatures des bois, des airs et des eaux se révoltent contre l'arrivée des étrangers. Ils ne nous veulent rien que du mal.»

Frère Arbre est grand et fort. Il est bon et sage. Il déclare:

«Cela vaut la peine d'accueillir les étrangers. Ils voyagent depuis très longtemps, par des sentiers qu'on n'a jamais vus. Ils peuvent partager avec nous leurs histoires, leurs espoirs... ils sont cousins de la flamme. Ils seront nos frères aussi, si on les reçoit amicalement! Il faut qu'on leur fasse confiance.»

Mais Frère Belette répond:

«C'est pas vrai. Ils ne nous parleront pas de leurs voyages, ni de comment devenir cousins du feu. Frère Raton Laveur vient de me dire que ces intrus sont meurtriers, qu'avec leur feu ils sont tortionnaires! Je ne veux pas perdre une minute de plus. Il faut qu'on prépare une défense contre eux, pour les renvoyer d'où ils viennent!»

Frère Belette court en direction du bruit, son courage feint est peu convaincant. Le grand arbre l'appelle, mais il ne répond pas. Frère Arbre est grand et sage. Le pouls des étrangers est tout proche. La pluie coule à flots autour de Frère Arbre.

Frère Arbre jette un coup d'oeil vers l'endroit par où sont passées les silhouettes il n'y a pas longtemps. Avec le jour qui tombe lentement et la pluie qui inonde la forêt, il est difficile de les voir s'avancer. Même sans les voir, Frère Arbre peut sentir la pulsation et entendre les salutations des nouveaux frères qui rebondissent sur les troncs des grands arbres et tombent dans les clairières en tourbillonnant.

Un grondement bas vient de la forêt au nord du grand arbre. Toutes les créatures s'agitent; le bruit toujours constant dicte la vitesse de l'agitation. Les bêtes aux yeux sauvages courent en furie, entre les arbres pour échapper à l'inévitable. Le battement de coeur les entoure. Les animaux féroces, et frénétiques, émergent en vagues des arbres et se battent à coups de griffes pour s'enfuir.

«Les animaux! Calmez-vous! N'ayez pas peur. Les étrangers sont nos frères. Ce battement est leur façon de nous saluer... Attendez! S'il vous plaît, ne vous en allez pas! Attendez! Ils sont nos frères!»

Soudain, le silence. Les animaux se figent, terrifiés. Même la pluie semble paralysée. Les chevreuils clignent de leurs longs cils noir. Les oiseaux semblent suspendus par les fils de pluie glacée. Un air de défaite gagne les yeux des animaux, des oiseaux, du grand arbre et de toutes les créatures de forêt.

Ils entrent, leurs pattes ne font pas de bruit. Ils sont armés de bâtons pointus et on voit la rage dans leurs yeux.

Le grand arbre sage et fort s'incline vers les nouveaux frères, abattu, vaincu par sa confiance. Les animaux se dispersent, indolents, la tête basse et le pas lent. Les oiseaux ne chantent plus. Les buissons pendent avec tristesse. Les nouveaux frères jettent le corps d'un jeune faon par terre, et créent la flamme avec les roches. La pluie tombe de tous côtés sans même toucher au petit groupe ni aux flammes.

L'arbre ferme ses grands yeux sages. Les êtres humains mettent le faon au feu et s'assoient par terre. Ils sont maintenant la source de tous bruits dans la forêt. La pluie pèse sur les branches du grand arbre fort.

Tout est froid et gris, sauf une larme chaude qui coule des yeux fermés de l'arbre, qui brille pour un moment, puis finit par se mêler à la pluie.

Le reflux du moment

To Find a Raven in the Fog

Gen Higgs

"A story, a story, Grandma, we want a story," cried the three children. Grandma sighed. It was well past bedtime already, and these three showed no sign of tiredness. Searching her memory for a good tale, she remembered something her son had shown her a week before. A dedicated anthropologist, he had shown her some old Spanish manuscripts describing Indian myths. One had particularly caught her attention.

"Well my dears, this story is about a girl named Mist between the Stars. In her language the name is very long, I don't think I can pronounce it properly, so I'll just call her Mist. She lived a long time ago a bit up the coast, where Daddy and Mommy took you on vacation last summer. In this story Mist had just been stolen by raiders, but she had managed to escape."

"How? Did she jump into a speedboat and zoom away?"

Grandma paused, "Well, I don't know exactly how she escaped. Remember, this happened a long time ago. It happened before speedboats and police, before any Europeans had come to Canada. But I do know that the thick fog that had crawled in helped her hide until the raiders had given up and gone home. Anyway, she was lost in the fog on an island that she didn't know...

Shivering violently, Mist grabbed a rock from the forest floor and threw it as far as she could. A faint crack of stone on stone echoing back through the thick fog was the only sign that it had reached the narrow beach below. The sound of the waves, barely thirty steps away, were strangely muffled, as were the shrieking cries of seagulls.

She longed to scream with them, but she was afraid that the raiders might hear. Things always echoed peculiarly in the fog. Choking back sobs, she tried to think of what to do. Nothing came to mind.

"No, this can't happen. I can't have escaped them just to get lost and get stuck on a moldy island!" Mist said to the tree trunk she was leaning against. She repeated her denial again, even more petulantly, but the tree showed no sign of caring. It seemed identical to all the other trees for as far as she could see, which wasn't very fair at all. Covered in green-grey lichen and branchless until far above her head, they were cold, silent pillars. Like everything else in the miserable place, they offered no hope of food or shelter.

When night came and rain began to fall, things started to look really bad. Hope that this was all a dream was vanishing. The constant patter of rain was too consistent; time too drawn out for it to be a warning dream come to her at night. Reality was bitter. She had escaped a life of captivity only to find herself lost, perhaps forever.

She wished she was at home, listening to the crackle of flames in the fire and her family quietly talking as she drifted off to sleep.

With a sick feeling inside, born of hunger and grief, she curled into a ball and tried to fall asleep at the roots of the tree she had been leaning on all day. It was hard because she was wet and cold and was not used to the nightime noises of the forest, but eventually weariness overcame fear.

The next three days seemed identical in their grey misery. She was afraid to forage very far in the thick fog, so all she could find to eat were some raw oysters and a few mushrooms. After a day of vomitting into the bushes she decided that eating the mushrooms was a risky idea. She had never paid attention to mushroom picking and the tasty ones looked all too similar to the poisonous ones. All the wood she could find was too soaked to burn so she was constantly cold; her nose was constantly running because she cried so much.

She spent most of her time leaning against her tree thinking of what she would have been doing back at home in the village. Life at home was hard, often filled with chores and compromises, but at least she was never so lonely. Even her gossiping aunts with their thousands of instructional stories and helpful hints would be welcome company right now.

When she awoke on the fifth day, Mist knew something had changed. The sun had broken through the clouds, and its light shone in muted rays through the forest ceiling. Everything had changed slightly. The land had become warmer; the moss was a thick emerald green, the earth richer, redder. Even the dead branches hung with ghostly ribbons like an old man's beard seemed to be more majestic than before.

When she went down to the ocean, the cold grey waves still crashed against the rocks. Spreading their salty spray and bubbly foam high into the air, they were still a barrier surrounding the island. Too far to swim to, but close enough to taunt her eyes the opposite shore sat mocking her. Less steep and with the occasional beach it seemed a far more pleasant place. Mist thought she had been there once before. If she was right about the island across the water, she knew what island she was on now. The steepest, most barren island in the area, and it was more than a day's paddle away from her village.

After sliding a few raw oysters down, and feeling their grit grind on her teeth, Mist decided to explore her situation. The lifting of the fog did not bring her much hope, but after sitting under a tree crying for so long she was ready to try. Even the tree was getting tired of her moaning.

As far as she could see in both directions there was a narrow strip of rocky beach exposed by the tide. Above it, endless trees reached up to the sky.

A point of land to one side blocked her vision, so she turned to go and see what was beyond it. Perhaps there would be some dry wood washed up high above the tide line by the last storm. Perhaps there would be a part of the forest where short plants and bushes grew instead of towering cedars.

The easiest time for her to make such a trip was when the tide was out, exposing the margin of shoreline. At high tide, the branches dipped into the waves and from the water line up was impassable forest. Although the islands looked like smooth walls reaching towards the sky from a canoe upon the water, they were actually broken cliffs disguised by a thick blanket of trees. While the trees could perch in narrow gullies and between boulders as large as longhouses, Mist could not.

Her only path was along the slimy rocks. The footing was treacherous; often she would fall off a wobbling rock or slide down the slick algae into worse filth. The sea meant life, providing food and a method of travel, but at its edge, the detritus of a rich marine ecology came to rest. By the time she reached the point her clothes were mottled green and brown with slime, the softly woven cedar torn in many places to expose tender skin to abrasion. She smelled like a dead seal.

When she reached the point, the land beyond was no different than the land behind. Tall trees still stretched to the sky, roots dipping almost into the sea. Seabirds and an eagle circled to their tops looking down on Mist. The birds called out; she didn't know whether they were laughing at her or crying. She sat down on a convenient rock.

There seemed to be no end to her string of bad luck. Overwhelmed at the thought of spending the rest of her life by herself she began to cry again.

"Why did this happen? Why was I down on the beach playing with the younger girls instead of helping the women with the weaving?". Once in a while she wondered if talking to herself meant that she was going crazy.

Through her tears she noticed something different on the beach ahead. It was far away, at the edge of her vision, but obviously too big to be a deer and too active to be a piece of driftwood. It was moving, which was a change from the stillness that had surrounded her for so long. She was afraid that it might be a bear, but cautiously crept a little closer.

When she had halved the distance she crouched behind a boulder to observe. Two bear cubs bouncing on a log like it was a teeter-totter. Mist was sad that it wasn't people. She wanted to go home, but the cubs antics quickly cheered her up. They seemed so full of joy, so clumsy and energetic she couldn't help staying to watch.

After a short while, the wind began to pick up, a cold fresh breeze began to push clouds over the sun. In the sudden cool, the back of Mist's neck rose in shivers. She noticed all of the birds had left except for one big black raven. It circled the bear cubs, then landed on a stretch of beach.

Suddenly a man's voice was carried to her ears by the wind.

"No, No, No! Gitsanuk, you stupid piece of rotten fish! I said push this side down. Down, not up. Do I have to do everything myself? Gitsaqeq, If you ever want to get this canoe off the rock, you are going to have to push down on your side just as hard. Are you both even shorter and lazier than you look?" The discourse continued without any sign of softening, but Mist had heard enough. Angry people were far better than no people, and the man had a humourous tone in his voice.

Bursting out of her hiding place she ran down the shore towards the people. The rocks were just as smelly and abrasive as before but she hardly looked down this time. Splashing putrid water and rousing clouds of gulls from their perches, she charged on.

When she reached the people, she stopped short. All three had turned to stare at her. She could see why she had mistaken them for bears; the two boys trying to free the log were nearly as stout as they were short. They were tanned deep brown; and as they scrambled over the rocks they bounced with energy. The third man was more sedate. He sat on a rock and presided over the efforts. He reminded Mist of a bird. He was a full head taller than she was and not at all skinny, but the way he sat with his feet tucked under him and quickly glanced about almost sideways was very birdlike. His hair, cropped fairly short, bunched and curled like oiled feathers gleaming black in the pale sunlight. After an uncomfortable silence, the man spat and said,

"Gitsanuk, what do think this is?" Mist looked down and realized how tattered she was. Even to these strangers, appeared on this barren shore, she must have presented a sorry sight. Gulping self-consciously she tried to speak. Her first words came out as a garbled croak, wrought with emotion. In the last few days she had thought a lot about being rescued, but had never worried that her rescuers might not be there for her or even want to help her.

"I was captured by raiders. They came to my village and stole me and some of the younger girls. I escaped when the fog came, but the little girls couldn't run as fast and got caught. Then they paddled away so I couldn't help them. And I was left here." Reflexively she reached up to comb her hair with her fingers, but not much could be done with the matted mess. She was quite sure that it, like everything else about her, had lost its healthy lustre. Nothing could be done about her filthy dress or pungent odour either.

"Abandoned eh? Why don't you come over here and help us get our canoe off the rocks? It's stuck thanks to Gitsanuk and Gitsaqeq and I'm scared that my beautiful craftsmanship might be ruined." Seeing her hesitation the man offhandedly added, "I guess, maybe we can help you somehow. You could come home with us if you want."

With that begrudging offer of help, she grittrd her teeth and came forward to help the two boys lift their canoe off the rocks. Being rude and refusing to help the strange group would not get her anywhere. Why they had come here, and who they were was a mystery.

Even the canoe was strange. Unlike other canoes, which were beautifully carved and finished, this canoe seemed half done. There was no figurehead animal on the front, and inside it had no spirit line and was so rough that it gave her slivers. It was more like a hollowed tree than a carefully wrought ship. She had often laughed at the men in her village for taking so much time on even the most trivial details, but this canoe made her feel uncomfortable. It was almost like a mishappen child.

Freeing the canoe from the rocks took almost all day. Gitsanuk had laughingly told her that their master had left it floating, tied to a tree, until the tide dropped and it got stuck. The large man, who Gitsaqeq whispered called himself Raven, did almost nothing. He shouted directions that did not help, and insults meant to encourage them to speed up. Eventually, when it was painfully obvious that his strength and height were needed, he stood up from the rock and finished the job single-handedly.

His strength was amazing. Mist had underestimated how strong he was when he was sitting. He was easily as strong as the strongest man in her village. He lifted the strange canoe on one shoulder and moved it by himself; but once it was free he left the two boys to drag it into the water.

Mist supposed that he must have been a powerful chief to consider himself so above such labour, but what kind of chief traveled in such a canoe, with only two boys as companions? Why would he stop on such a desolate shore? When she asked him his only reply was to laugh and say,

"Yes, I'm very powerful, little woman-to-be." Raven stopped to give himself an admiring glance, "It's obvious, isn't it? And the only reason we stopped on this miserable island was because of the fog got lost in. I've never seen fog so thick. Sitting out in a canoe, fishing, is fine for a day, but we got stuck out there for what seems like a month." He looked at her with calculating eyes and finished, "Of course, if my unfinished boat isn't good enough, you can stay here instead of coming home with us."

Mist's shudder was enough of a reply. She would do anything to live in a village again. Skulking around in the forest eating raw shellfish was horrible. The dried fish they shared with her reminded her of home so much she almost started to cry again. When the three men left the island, she went with them in their precarious canoe.

Apprehension and choppy waves made her stomach roll the whole way. Gitsanuk had told her that the three of them were living by themselves in an abandoned village that used to be inhabited by Raven's family. He also hinted that ever mentioning his family to Raven was a very bad idea. He told her that, all the joking was gone from his voice and he seemed very sad.

That made Mist nervous, how could she carry on a conversation without ever mentioning his family? She was also nervous because she had never been a good cook, craftsman, or seamstress, due to the fact that she had always preferred to play rather than help the women with chores. Even when she had been far too old to spend all her time like a child she had ignored all the pointed hints her family gave her and went off on her own. It had always been too easy to disappear when dinner had to be cooked, or tools repaired. Now she didn't know how she was going to repay Raven for rescuing her from the desolate island.

When they reached the village, it was twilight, and the purple sunset put everything in a strange light. It reminded Mist of a recurring dream she had had when she was a very small girl. In the dream she had stood on a beach at sunset and thrown a clamshell into the water. Only after the clamshell had disappeared beneath the waves would she realize that she had put something important in it. She would always run into the water and search for it, but there were too many clamshells for her to tell which one was hers.

Even without the unsettling remembrance of her dream, the village was eerie. There were four longhouses standing, but the bush was beginning to encroach upon them. Blackberry creepers and grass twined their way through the greyed wood, and saplings were growing in two of the houses' doorways. The beach in front of the houses was deserted, no other canoes were pulled up. Unlike Mist's village, no children could be heard playing; no old men rested in front of the longhouses carving; and no welcoming smoke rose from the houses.

She sniffed the air but instead of wood smoke and drying fish she smelt the musty scent of sun on old wood. Inside the longhouses it was worse. Strips of fading light shone between the boards, dividing up the hollow space. Where she would have expected to see sleeping mats and storage boxes of many people, there were only the belongings of the three men strewn about. Without the comfortable hum of people moving about their daily business, the place seemed cold and empty.

That evening, after her first cooked meal in days, Mist felt much better. The silence, almost natural in the forest, was eerie and laden with ghosts here, but she could get used to it. She felt much better after washing and borrowing some clean clothes from Gitsanuk. Although his clothes did not fit her well because she was taller and more slender than he was, they were dry and warm. Even Raven began to behave better. Although he sent her to gather firewood with a perfunctory sweep of his hand he was becoming almost courteous.

As they relaxed by the fire Raven told her stories of his adventures. Whether they were entirely false or just hugely exaggerated she wasn't sure, but she didn't want to be rude so she didn't interrupt. She burst into laughter many times as Gitsanuk looked on bored, and Gitsaqeq fell asleep. Obviously they had heard the stories too many times to care.

In each story Raven would be hilariously smart and steal something from someone more powerful. He seemed delighted by his own trickiness, and often would remark on how clever a particular plan had been. He always laughed at his own jokes, and if she did not, he would explain them to her until she did. She didn't see any of the things he said he had taken, which either disproved his stories entirely, or proved his claim that he had always given them to the people of his village.

Whether the stories were true or not, Mist could see Raven was benefiting enormously from the attention. By the end of his second story he was far less obscene. By the end of the third he even asked her what she thought. When he told his stories his face would become animated, his gestures exaggerated. In the flickering firelight it seemed as if he were wearing a ceremonial mask and dancing. His tall tales reminded her of the stories that were told at potlatches.

When she had almost dozed off, lulled by the comforting crackle of the fire, Raven stopped gesticulating and looked directly at her. In the dark she could see his eyes gleaming craftily from under his mop of jet-black hair.

"So do you think your family survived the raid?" He said. "Mine didn't. I left for an extended halibut fishing trip with the two slaves I had recently captured, and when I got back my family was dead. If there were any survivors they must have scattered. But I'll get my revenge."

Mist felt sad. She didn't want revenge; she wanted to find the people she loved alive and well.

"I don't know. As they dragged me into the canoe, I could hear so many people screaming and yelling. I couldn't tell but I thought I heard my father yelling and then he suddenly stopped." She said, curling up into a ball and hugging her knees as tightly as she could. "I want to go home, Raven."

"Well little woman-to-be, that isn't as easy as it sounds. I have a better idea. I need a wife to take care of me, and you need a man to take care of you and a place to live. I don't suppose you would mind an informal trade? I could make you a wealthy woman. If not I will be glad to drop you back off where I found you "As Mist indignantly jumped up he continued, "Come on, many girls would jump at a chance to get their claws in someone as smart as me. Feel free to think it over, though. I can see how you might feel a bit giddy. A girl like you probably never thought she would have any say in the matter. Just don't make me wait too long."

A little while later, as she hid in the farthest corner of the longhouse, Mist thought over Raven's bizarre question. She never had expected that someone would propose to her. A girl's family always considered the matter for her. It was wrong, marrying a strange man without her family's knowledge, without their permission. Not only was it completely against custom, it was probably unwise. How could she know whether Raven would make a good match? She had never been married before, unlike her parents, who could use their experience to decide. But she had always felt that her people had too many rules concerning respectful behavior. Was this her chance to free herself from those rigid rules? Or was this just wrong?

She couldn't go back to being lost on that island. It was a fate worse than death, and just might turn out to be death as well. Raven's jokes and stories showed a kind side to him. Her timely rescue from the beach left her feeling grateful. Raven was even respected by Gitsanuk and Gitsaqeq. They seemed to care about each other. She couldn't just informally marry Raven, though. She didn't like some parts of custom, but that was going too far.

She was torn between choosing one or the other, but two memories clinched the decision. She remembered when Grandmother, a very wise woman, had called for her when she was very ill. The old woman had clutched her hand, death rattling in her throat, and had said,

"Child, you are a stubborn one. No, it's not a bad thing. It is your hidden strength. Just remember to look at what you are being so obstinate for." With that her eyes closed for the last time, resting until death carried her away.

She also remembered her recurring dream about the clamshell. She knew now that her family and village were inside that clamshell, and if she threw it away now she would never get it back.

"No I shouldn't do it, can't do it, won't do it. I don't care if it means I'd be married to a powerful man. I'll just have to say, No." She decided.

When she told Raven the next morning, he was decidedly displeased.

"Does everybody think they're too good for me today? Come on you two bumble-buts, we've got work to do." He shouted at Gitsanuk and Gitsaqeq and he stormed through the door. Apologetically they shrugged as they hurried after Raven. Gitsaqeq quickly murmured that Raven was a bit stubborn, but after pouting a while he would be helpful. Then he grabbed his hat and ran.

Mist had decided the night before that the only way she might be able to convince Raven that he wanted to help her get home was to soften him up a bit. She began to do the work she had shirked at home with a vengeance. Cleaning the longhouse, repairing tools that had become broken and replenishing the firewood pile were a start.

She also began to prepare the four of them her favorite meal, salmon and blackberries. Luckily both were in season, but still, preparing the meal was hard work. She wished she had spent more time at home learning how to do such things.

The sun was shining brightly again, as if to match her mood. As she was picking blackberries she became more and more confident that her plan to win Raven's acceptance through his stomach would work. In the distance she could hear waves crashing, birds calling, Raven yelling and occasionally a call or joke from the other two. She wondered why they were always so quick to obey him. He had stolen them from their village the same way the raiders had tried to steal her. She would never stay away from her village like them, though.

By evening, her meal would have made her aunt who loved to cook proud. She waited with anticipation as the three men came in. They looked tired and strained but Gitsanuk and Gitsaqeq perked up immediately. Raven, however, was brooding.

"What is this?" he asked as he took his first bite. "It's not very good, I could do much better" he concluded. Wisely, Mist held her tongue, although it was a struggle. She noticed that although he continued to insult the salmon he ate faster and faster. Long after she had finished eating, Raven continued to gorge on the meal. She had never seen anyone eat so much, or so messily, even at feasts.

When he was done, Raven sat next to the fire, idly playing with fishbones and then throwing them into the coals. When she had had enough of the acrid smoke, Mist grabbed all of the skeleton that was left and without a word took it back to the stream where Gitsanuk had caught it from. Guiltily she hoped that there were enough bones left for the salmon to return to its home in the sea.

When she had asked Gitsanuk to get the fish for her he had looked dubious and almost said something. After taking much longer than she expected he returned with a moderately sized fish. The odd thing was that he had seemed amazed that he had found any salmon in the stream.

When she returned, Raven eyed her speculatively. She could tell that he was planning something because the cruel, cunning look had returned. Hurriedly she turned away. To avoid looking at him she pretended to go to sleep.

Later on that night, she awoke with a shock. Raven had snuck up behind her and slipped his hand over her mouth. Paralyzed with fear she lay there as he whispered to her

"Little woman-to-be, do you know how to build a smoke house?"

Feeling her terrified nod, he continued, "That's good. My boys and I will be away for a few days. We're leaving now. Have one made by the time we get back. We're going to be smoking salmon, sweet thing." His putrid fish breath almost made her gag. Obviously he hadn't cleaned his teeth with a cedar brush like she did every night. "I don't have time now, but don't worry, I'll convince you to marry me later. No woman ever refuses me forever. Just be a good little woman-to-be and have the smokehouse ready when I get back. Oh yes, and next time, don't throw away the fishbones until I'm done with them."

As he left, Mist shuddered.

Although she didn't get any more sleep that night, she was up by dawn the next morning constructing the smokehouse. The threat in Raven's words the night before was barely concealed. Barely stopping to eat, for two days she worked on it, but she was small and clumsy. Progress was very slow. On the third day, she was desperately afraid that Raven would come home, and she had it only half done.

The problem was that he was so unpredictable. His mood changed more often than she could keep track of. His family must have had a tough time getting along with him, she thought, in spite of his random kindness.

She just needed a little more time.

She dug deep into her memory and remembered that her grandmother had had the ability to call fog. Shamanism ran in families, so maybe she could call fog as well. It was a big risk, but she was more afraid of what might happen if Raven arrived before the smokehouse was ready than of angering the spirits by asking for things ungratefully. She had always tried to be respectful. Hopefully, if she did the ritual correctly, the spirits would forgive her even if they didn't help her.

To call fog required a specific ceremony that Mist remembered watching as a child. It never varied. Her grandmother always the same things in the same order. She didn't have exactly the same materials as her grandmother but Mist decided the words and respect were the most important things.

What resulted that night was heavy cloud cover. Mist wasn't sure whether or not it was due to her devices, but she didn't want to bother the spirits by asking too many times.

The next day, by working frantically, she finished the smokehouse. Her hands were blistered and full of slivers, and her back felt permanently twisted, but she had finished. She didn't know that she could do anything like that.

Shortly afterwards, Gitsanuk, Gitsaqeq and Raven returned. They brought back many times more salmon than she expected. Only a few had come to the stream near the longhouses so early in the season. Instead of being proud of their catch, they were angry and confused though. Raven loudly said,

"Good thing we're back without being caught. Last night I tried to find our way, but Gitsaqeq got us lost. The clouds covered the stars and blocked out all light. We might as well have had our eyes closed for all that they helped us. I hope you got your work done, little woman."

He noticed her sudden smile but didn't comment.

The next few days consisted of backbreaking labour for Gitsanuk and Gitsaqeq. Mist felt sorry for them, but was too busy herself to help. Raven had them gathering wood for the smokehouse and tending it non-stop. He never helped, but constantly berated them. Finally Mist had enough,

"Can you stop being so foul-mouthed? Everyone is tired of listening to your voice. No wonder there are so few salmon in the stream here. They probably left because they didn't want to hear you anymore. And when are you going to return the salmon bones to their stream? They can't return home when you have their bones rotting in a pile beside our house." She said in a cold voice, too angry to have caution.

His blow caught her by surprise. It almost seemed as if she had instantaneously been moved to the floor. She was too stunned to cower when he came to stand over her.

"My foul mouth was the first you ever heardfrom me, little woman-to-be. If you didn't like it you shouldn't have followed me home. Go back to your island if you like, carpies aren't welcome here. And the fishbones are mine, all mine. I have plans for them." He spat. "I get what I want so don't get in my way."

Mist didn't say anything, but when he fell asleep that night she filled the hollowed out log with a quarter of the smoked salmon and prepared to return to the island. As she got ready to leave, she thought that in the dark corner where Raven slept she could see him sitting, watching. With all the bumping and crashing as she tried to sneak around, a man as sharply observant as Raven couldn't have stayed asleep. He didn't say anything to stop her.

It took her twelve days to find her village. She had never paddled even a small canoe before. When she got back, her family was overjoyed to have her back. They noticed that she was not the spoiled child she had been when she was captured. Her father, who had been hit on the head, was otherwise unharmed. Many of the other villagers were hurt or gone though.

While they feasted that night, some of the men told a strange tale of salmon stolen from a neighboring village's stream by three men in the dead of night. When the men of the village had caught them in the act a second time they followed the three back to a deserted village full of stinking fish remains and hordes of fleas. Repelled by the insects, the village men left as quickly as they could without investigating further.

"Grandma, why were there bugs? We don't have bugs inside our house, except when Steve brings them in." One of the drowsy children asked.

Grandma laughed gently as she tucked them in,

"Of course not, we don't have piles of fishbones for the bugs to eat either. Now sleep dear."

"What about Raven, did he get bitten to death by the fleas?" Steve, the most kind hearted of the three children asked.

"No, Raven must have escaped because there are many, many stories about him. Now go to sleep."

The Hero

Lindsay Chung

A biting wind stung Apostolos Valerianos's plump cheeks as he trudged toward the bar, hands stuffed deep in the pockets of his pants. He shuffled along, his face cast downward trying to shield himself from the insistent rain pouring out of the starless Mediterranean sky.

As he approached the familiar wooden establishment, Apostolos smiled slightly. He could already see the bright candlelight of the bar, hear the bartender calling to him and taste the refreshing Retsina wine. He shook the water from his full, white hair and pushed open the door.

Apostolos blinked as his eyes adjusted to the brilliance of the bar. He looked around and beamed, his eyes falling upon smiling men and women seated at round, wooden tables talking amiably over drinks. White candles cast whimsical shadows on their faces and all around the room. He walked slowly to the counter and was embraced by the atmosphere of the bar.

"Apostolos!" a deep voice cried, "you're back! Come, have a drink old man!"

A round, dark face popped up from behind the counter, and the man grinned at Apostolos, his dark brown eyes twinkling.

"Hello Alexi," Apostolos said, "I'll have Retsina."

"Anything for you, my friend." Alexi danced over to the bottles and poured his good friend a large glass of wine.

Apostolos took his glass and looked thoughtfully around the room. As he sipped his drink, his dark eyes focused on a group of younger men talking in the corner.

"Did you see the new girl at the store?" one of the men asked, smoothing his black mustache. The others laughed, and as they drank, Apostolos could hear the clinking of their glasses.

Apostolos took his jacket off and sighed happily. It was nice to be back in this familiar old place. Candlelight danced off the vivid purples and blues of the painting on the nearest wall.

"You know, I've always loved that painting," he said.

The man beside him turned, his brown eyes cloudy and vague. "Yah," he murmured absently, his breath reeking of alcohol.

"Hey Apostolos! You want another one?" Alexi cried, reaching out his long arm to take the empty glass in front of Apostolos.

"Sure."

"You were gone for such a long time that I worried you would never come back," Alexi said loudly, his back turned to Apostolos.

Apostolos sighed angrily, his dark eyes clouding over for a minute.

"Well, if the damned Spanish government had kept its word, I would have been home a lot sooner."

"What are you talking about? You can't be talking nonsense now. You've only had one drink." Alexi laughed. "Don't tell me you've become soft in your old age." He clapped Apostolos heartily on the back.

"Of course I'm not talking nonsense," Apostolos cried, his cheeks flushed, "the government owes me a lot."

"Whatever you say," Alexi replied, turning back to his work.

Apostolos took a sip of his wine and glared at the wooden counter. He ran his hand along the grain of the wood, deep in thought.

Black shoes flew up in the air as the man beside him fell over backward. Hearing the thump of the wooden chair hitting the floor, Apostolos turned around and stared, shocked, at the man. A stunned silence swept the place as all conversations stopped.

Suddenly, Apostolos burst out laughing, a loud, guttural and jolly sound that echoed through the room. He continued laughing, his dark eyes twinkling, as he bent over to help the young man.

Once Apostolos began to laugh, the sound spread through the room. The other patrons began to laugh and cheer before resuming their conversations.

"Are you okay?" Apostolos asked, extending an arm to the crumpled and embarrassed man.

"Oh sure," the man said bashfully, "I'm just a little drunk."

Apostolos laughed. "I'd say so."

"Thanks a lot." The young man smiled. "I'd have stayed there forever if you didn't help." He picked up his chair and sat down, resuming his drinking. "I'm Aristotle." He held out a smooth, slender, dark hand toward Apostolos.

"I'm Apostolos, " he said, smiling as he shook Aristotle's hand.

Alexi came back. "Hey Kid, thanks for the entertainment, " he said, laughing, "I sure saved a lot of money on the comedian I was going to have come tonight." He patted Aristotle's dark, curly hair and laughed again."These young lads just can't drink like we can, wouldn't you agree, Apostolos?" Alexi winked at Apostolos and walked back to pour a drink for another customer.

Apostolos took a sip of his drink and let the various sounds of the bar wash over him. He heard men and women talking and laughing loudly, and he could even hear someone singing. He turned around for a minute and saw a large man belting out a popular operatic tune, the men and women around him clapping and dancing.

Apostolos brought his attention back to his drink and relaxed in his chair. He glanced up and noticed his reflection in the mirror behind the counter. Apostolos sat captivated by the image in front of him, unable to believe what he saw. He rubbed his hand over his stubbly chin and sighed thoughtfully. Did he really have that many wrinkles in his forehead? When had all of his hair gotten so white? He took another sip of his wine and sighed again.

A rush of cool air swept through the bar as the heavy wooden door opened. Sandals clicked along the floor as two people walked into the room.

Apostolos turned around and watched as a tall, old man stopped and looked around, running a large hand through his silver hair. He coughed and bent to say something to the beautiful woman beside him. Apostolos couldn't take his eyes off the woman as she threw back her head in laughter, her long, thick black hair cascading down her back. The candlelight illuminated her large, dark brown eyes, and Apostolos watched carefully as the woman and her companion sat down at a table. So close that he thought she could hear his rapidly beating heart.

Apostolos turned back to the counter and sat amazed by the tidal wave of desire that swept over him. As he sat sipping his wine, Apostolos thought of the woman. She was, by far, the most beautiful woman he had ever seen. Though she showed no signs of graying hair or wrinkles, Apostolos figured that the woman was around forty years old. While he'd only seen her for a moment, Apostolos found her to be incredibly alluring. He took a sip of his wine, savoring the dry taste. Why would a wonderful woman like her be the slightest bit interested in an old man like him? Apostolos' thoughts swirled angrily like the harsh winter's wind outside. To her, he was probably just a lonely old man sipping wine in a bar. What if she knew he was a ship's pilot? What if she knew about his discovery? Would she be impressed? How could he let her know about his exciting past?

Apostolos turned to Aristotle. "Hey Aristotle! Have you ever been outside of Greece?"

"Only to Turkey," Aristotle answered, lifting his head off the counter. He tried desperately to hold his head up as he squinted at Apostolos. "Why? Have you?"

Apostolos raised his voice a little. "I sure have. I've been away from home since 1590," he paused expectantly, "and I actually just returned from Spain."

"Wow, " Aristotle whistled, "I'm impressed. What did you do?"

"I was a ship's pilot. " Apostolos looked in the mirror but was disappointed to see that the woman was not paying attention to him. He raised his voice slightly. "I went on a couple of expeditions for Spain. I was sent by the Viceroy of Mexico to find the North-West Passage."

The sound of glass hitting the counter stopped Apostolos. Aristotle blinked and picked up his glass, smiling sheepishly.

"The North-West Passage?" Aristotle's olive skin came together in deep wrinkles of thought as he wrestled feebly with the name.

"Yes, everyone, especially the British, wanted to find that passage because it would improve trade." Apostolos eyes twinkled with the memories, and he smiled brightly. "But I found it, and now the Spanish can rub that in the British faces!"

"The Spanish!" Alexi cried as he refilled Apostolos glass. "Imagine an Apostolos Valerianos sailing for the Spanish! You must have had to change your name. I bet they gave you some crazy name like John the Greek." He laughed heartily. "Imagine that!" he cried, shaking his head as he left to serve another customer.

"You found the North-West Passage?!" Aristotle cried loudly. "Wow!"

"I did, and it's amazing. I'm the first person who has seen it." Apostolos looked up proudly and noticed with satisfaction that the beautiful woman was listening to his conversation. "I sailed with a small Caravela and a Pinnace from Nova Spania along the western coast of the West Indies of Spain for what seemed like ages," he continued, his voice rising with excitement. "Our boats were small, and the voyage was incredibly dangerous." Apostolos lowered his voice a bit as he became aware of another man pulling up a chair beside him. "I could have died. The winds were treacherous, and we had to guard ourselves against sickness."

"Oh yes," the Arabic man sitting beside Apostolos nodded wisely. "When on the sea, one must be careful to eat right. I've heard many stories of mariners who have died on long expeditions."

"Yes, anyway, some days the waves rose as high as our boats. There were times when I was sure that we would capsize. The dampness was overwhelming; I could never get warm. The water was rough. Waves threw our boats around like toys. Many men got seasick. We sat in our boats for weeks, pale ghosts searching for something indescribable." Apostolos felt someone's warm breath on the back of his neck as he realised that more and more people were listening to his story. Men and women were cluttered around him, their eyes riveted on Apostolos as his adventure rolled along, the excitement building like a strong wave rising to a crescendo of foam and salt water. Apostolos took a sip of his wine and closed his eyes for a second. When he opened them again, Aristotle was inches from his face.

"Well?" he asked impatiently.

"The weather was so bad that we couldn't see where we were going. Our boats were bombarded by rain. The wind was horrible, more powerful than anything you'll ever feel. With a bit of luck, I was able to steer us in the right direction. Everyone was depending on me to find this passage. Younger men would have fallen under the pressure; but with over forty years of experience, I knew I could deal with it. I wasn't worried. I felt that we were getting closer to the passage every day. I can't tell you how I knew; I just did. After all these difficult weeks of sailing, I woke up one morning. It was still very windy, and I could taste the salt from the ocean in every breath that I took. Yet, for the first time in days, it wasn't raining. As I strained to keep my breakfast down, I realised that the horizon looked different. The air tasted and smelled different; I knew I had come to something important. Sunlight danced off the low-lying clouds; and for an instant, I saw a broad inlet. The lack of rain seemed to signal the start of our good fortune. I calculated the inlet to be around forty seven degrees of latitude. I sprang quickly into action and told my mariners to follow me into this incredible expanse of sea."

A chair clinked behind Apostolos; and in the mirror, he saw the beautiful woman sitting behind him. She rested her head on her slim, olive arms as she leaned toward him, completely enthralled by his story. Apostolos smiled to himself and took another sip of his wine. As he looked toward the mirror again, Apostolos noticed that the old man who had come in with the woman was scowling at him. He shrugged as he received a new glass of wine.

"As we turned to enter the inlet, the wind began to let up and I noticed some fog ahead. I looked around. I knew that we had found something special. The fog crystals in the air were like pieces of silver being thrown through the sky; it was truly magical. At the entrance to the inlet, I saw a tall spired rock on a great island. Already, I could smell the fresh grass and cedar trees on land. We brought our boats in as close to this land as we could. I could almost touch the cold, smooth rock." He paused, hearing only the ragged breathing of the men and women in the bar.

"The wind began to pick up as we continued sailing, passing many islands. The powerful waves pushed us so close to shore that we almost hit bottom a few times. Once, the bow of our boat was heading straight at the rocky coast of a large island. Sweat poured down my face as we moved closer and closer to the island. At the last second, I was able to steer our boat away. My heart pounded wildly in my chest as the side of our little Caravela just barely passed by the island, narrowly missing the rocks."

Apostolos heard a few amazed whispers and exclamations, and he smiled happily.

"My men and I sailed for more than twenty days up this glorious passage. I woke up one particularly nasty day to find that two of my men had died the night before. I'm not sure how they died, though I had been noticing that both men were very weak and had complained of gum problems. I found them lying on the bottom of the boat, their bodies as cold as ice. Now, I've been doing this for forty years, and I've seen a lot of men die. But let me tell you this: it is always hard to throw a man overboard and watch his lifeless body drift away in its watery grave." Apostolos took a deep breath.

"Well, after this difficult day, we decided to go ashore. After anchoring our battered boats and swimming to shore, I led my men toward the Garden of Eden. My feet on solid earth once more, I felt like I really was in paradise. The land was very rich and fruitful with glorious green grass and big, sturdy trees. We walked around for a few minutes, savoring each step we took with the dirt and grass beneath our feet and breathing in the musky smell of cedar trees. We all ran around like children, the wind whistling in our ears. Up we went, walking happily to the top of a grassy hill. I stopped in surprise at the top. Close enough to touch was a group of savages wearing only animal skins. A few of my men called out in surprise and started to turn back, but I commanded them to stop. I couldn't take my eyes off these wild men.

They stared back at me with dark eyes full of pride and confidence but didn't move. They stood there silently, their long, dark hair blowing behind them in the wind. A few minutes passed, and neither of us moved. I looked into their dark, weathered faces and read the stories written there. I saw their strength and resilience, and I finally decided to back away. We had no weapons, and besides, we'd come here to find the passage, not fight the savages."

Someone coughed, and Apostolos brought his mind back to the bar. He ran his hand along the counter and paused for a minute. He looked at all of the people gathered around him: old men in traditional clothing, young men and women in more modern garments, and men working in the bar. Heads full of grey, white and black hair faced Apostolos, eager to hear the end of his story.

Apostolos grinned and leaned back in his chair. "We went on land a few other times, more cautious than before. It was amazing over there, a lot like Nova Spania but not as warm. The land seemed to be rich in pearls, gold and silver. It was exciting, but everyone was anxious to get home. We finally reached the wide North Sea. We entered this strait, cold and tired sailors on our way home. We sailed these seas for many days in the fierce wind and rain, finally reaching the familiar waters around Nova Spania. With the proud knowledge that we had discovered the undiscoverable, we returned to the port of Acapulco. Walking on the wonderful Nova Spania soil, we clapped each other on the back, rejoicing and cheering. We felt like kings returning from a successful conquest. We clapped our grimy hands together, eager to tell others of our amazing discovery."

"Wow!" a group of men cheered loudly.

"Apostolos! You old dog!" Alexi cried, candlelight reflecting off his large, white teeth. "You're a hero! You really found the North-West Passage?"

"Yes, I did." Apostolos finished off his glass of wine. "People have been searching for this passage for years, and I found it. After forty years of exploration, I found the great passage!"

Apostolos heard the sound of dozens of hands clapping together, skin meeting with skin in a roar.

"You're amazing!"

"You're a hero!"

"You're the best!"

In a thundering wave of noise, Apostolos felt himself being lifted out of his chair. He looked down, surprised, as four tall men lifted him above their shoulders. Men reached out, hoping to touch the flesh of a hero. They cheered loudly as Apostolos was carried toward the door. The patrons of the bar left their drinks and ran alongside the men carrying Apostolos, crying out his name.

High above the heads of the men and women, Apostolos basked in his glory. He smiled and laughed as he was carried to the door, swaying slightly like a seagull on a stormy day.

A couple of women ran eagerly to the door, their skirts swirling around their dark, shapely legs. They held the door open as Apostolos was carried into the evening.

Outside, Apostolos heard the sound of an old man's voice. "Stop!" the voice cried frantically, "stop right now!"

The boisterous group of men and women stopped, rain pouring down on them. They helped Apostolos down. He took a moment to steady himself and then walked to the front of the group. Apostolos blinked, surprised to see the old man who had come in with the beautiful woman standing in front of him. He looked around and saw the beautiful woman standing off in a dark spot, away from everyone. Apostolos watched her for a minute as rain fell on her attractive body.

The man crossed his arms over his chest and glared, six feet of confidence and pride.

"What do you want?" Apostolos asked angrily. "How dare you talk to us like this?"

The man glared at him.

"Who do you think you are?" he spat angrily at Apostolos. "You come in here and tell us you found the North-West Passage and expect us to believe you." He swept an arm angrily toward the crowd of people. "And you! Why are you treating this dirty old man like a hero? Do you really believe him? Take a look at him! He's a withered, drunken old man!"

The men and women were silent as they looked from Apostolos to the tall, old man. Rain hit the ground and wind howled, but still no one spoke. Apostolos held his head high and squared his shoulders.

"You're rather old yourself."

The taller man laughed cruelly. "Perhaps, but with age I have learned not to be as gullible as you might like me to be. If you really discovered this North-West Passage, why are you here in a little Greek bar? Where is your medallion or your chest full of gold? If you really did discover the passage that everyone has been looking for, wouldn't we have heard about it?"

"I was supposed to get a reward. I even went to the King of Spain to get it."

"You were supposed to get a reward?! Where is it?"

"I haven't gotten it yet. The Spanish promised me rewards, but they aren't ready yet."

"So, you're saying it's their fault you aren't rich? Maybe they just didn't believe you!"

"Of course they believed me! Why else would they promise rewards? Why wouldn't they believe me? Why would I make this up?"

"Because you are an insecure old man who wants people to think he's a hero!"

"How dare you?!"

"How dare you ? Do you really expect us to believe you?"

"Yes! I'm an honest man."

"No, you're not. You are dishonest and dishonorable."

"Do you attack my honour, sir?" Apostolos cried angrily.

"I do not attack what does not exist."

"I demand satisfaction, sir."

"I will not fight with a drunkard; however, if you can prove your claim, you may have the hand of my daughter Athena," the man said haughtily, gesturing toward the beautiful woman who had captivated Apostolos attention earlier in the evening.

"I'm staying at the farm one mile north of here. Come to see me there tomorrow morning at eight o'clock, and I will give you your proof." Apostolos stalked away, shoulders rigid with pride and anger.

As Apostolos silhouette receded into darkness, Athena's father turned to the men and women standing across from him. "Well, I'd say that's the last we've seen of him. There's no way that he can prove his story." He laughed. "Come on, Athena," he said, pulling her to him and turning around.

As sunshine fell through the window in Athena's tiny room, she pulled on her jacket and skirt. She had begun to do her hair when there was a knock at her door.

"Athena," her father said, watching his daughter comb her long black hair, "what are you doing?"

"I'm getting ready. If I'm going to be the prize in this bet, I want to be there to see what happens."

"You have a lot of work to do at home; you should stay."

"And you should not have used me like this." Athena looked her father in the eyes. "Please let me come; it would only be fair."

Her father stared at her for a moment, seeing the stubborn lift of her chin and knowing that he could not refuse her.

"Fine. We are leaving in a minute; get your shoes on."

The early morning sunshine glinted off of Athena's dark hair as she closed the front door behind her. She pulled her jacket closer to her slim body and looked up at her father. "Do you have to do this? Why don't you just leave that man alone?"

"He is a dishonourable liar who will say anything to impress people, and those sorry fools at the bar just ate it all up. I want to expose him for what he is – a fraud."

"What if he does have proof? Why did you bet me as a prize?"

"Don't worry Athena. He will not have any proof."

Athena sighed as they walked toward the farm. Her father kept his eyes focused on the farm up ahead, but she looked around. Her big, bright eyes took in the proud olive trees and the mountains in the distance. She smiled as they passed a herd of sheep grazing in the field.

A few minutes later, Athena and her father came to a tiny wooden barn-house. Athena's father raised his arm and knocked loudly on the door. As his fist met the wood, the door fell open slightly.

"Hello?" Athena's father called. He listened intently but heard nothing. "Hello? Is anyone here?" He paused for a moment and then pushed the door open.

"He must be sleeping. Maybe we should just go home," Athena said softly.

Her father didn't answer. A rush of cold air swept over him, and a shiver ran through his body.

"Hello?" he called, more loudly this time. A strange silence hung in the air, making him feel uneasy. He turned and looked at his daughter. Athena looked back at him, confusion evident on her beautiful face.

"Can you hear me?" Athena's father called, stepping into the house. "Is anyone here?" He paused for a minute, looking around at the barren little house. It was empty as far as he could see. He took a few more steps into the house.

As the sun shone in through the open door, his eyes moved around the single room. They moved up and down the empty walls. They took in the empty chair and the clothes on the floor. They moved along slowly, finally falling upon Apostolos still body on the floor beside the bed.

"Oh!" he cried and hurried quickly toward Apostolos body. He bent down and shook Apostolos shoulders. "Hello? Can you hear me?" When there was no answer, Athena's father checked Apostolos pulse. He shuddered. He couldn't take his eyes off of Apostolos calm face. Not finding signs of life, he stood up.

Athena entered the room. She gasped when she saw Apostolos body. She looked up, shocked, and her wide eyes met those of her father. "Oh no," she uttered, "is he, is he... dead?"

"Yes." Her father nodded gravely. "He must have died in his sleep. I see no signs of blood or anything."

They stood there for a moment, unsure of their next move. Athena spotted a piece of paper lying on the floor beside Apostolos lifeless body.

"What's that?" she asked, her soft voice quivering.

Her father bent to pick it up. He turned the thin sheet of paper over and noticed that it was a letter.

"From Micheal Lok in Britain," he read. "My dearest friend Juan de Fuca, I have been talking to some friends of mine here in Britain, and they are very interested in hearing about your discovery of the North-West Passage."

The paper shook in his hand, and he fell back into the chair beside him. Stunned, he placed his head in his hands and closed his eyes.

Nootka Nirvana

Geoffrey Trotter

Mighty masts rose purposefully from the superstructure. Standing at attention, they professed the greatness of England to all whose eyes came to rest upon their magnificence. Every sail, securely bound to its mast with strong cords, was poised to be lowered in an instant at the Captain's command. A latticework of hemp ropes, incomprehensible to any untrained eye, criss-crossed in a pageant of precision and purpose as if patterned after the sailors aboard the vessel.

Two of these men were hunched over the bow guard rail, far below the crow's nest of the 100 foot ship as it swung lazy, sweeping arcs on its anchor.

"Better get yourself back to the captain's quarters before tea time there Chip," said Steven in his casual, gravelly voice as he planed down the newly installed board, sending the invigorating smell of freshly incised wood in as many directions as the chips, "I can handle the rest myself, thanks for your help."

Chip, a cabin boy of thirteen, looked up at his friend's face to catch the smile which was always there when the carpenter spoke. Satisfied with the friendly look, he scampered off to Captain Vancouver's cabin as best he could with his stiff, uncooperative, scar-ridden leg - the lasting reminder of nearly fatal lacerations sustained in the factory five years earlier. Since the ship had arrived back at Yuquot in Nootka Sound after months of mapping and circumnavigating the larger island to the East, he had been told to check for orders roughly every hour. As he passed the thick, stout mast, Chip looked upwards as he always did when on deck. Thrusting strongly upwards, in stark contrast to the weak sky above, the mast always made Chip feel significant to be a part of something as great as the King's Royal Navy.

The captain glanced up, then back down to the map he was labelling as Chip slipped past the worn door to the chart room. The captain had spent most of the last few days perched like an owl over his maps, the product of the previous months toil. "You're late," he sighed as he measured a distance on the map unrolled before him with the sharp-tipped dividers and compared it with the scale, finding it to be unsatisfactory.

"Yes sir, sorry sir, I was helping fix the rail at the bow where it was starting to rot away. Steve said he couldn't have done it without me. It was a two man lift to get the board in position, and..." The captain's eyes bore into him, instantly Chip fell silent.

"I want you to take this over to the Spanish boat. It is an invitation for Captain Quadra to come aboard tomorrow to discuss the treaty."

"The treaty," thought Chip. It was such a grand thing! The Spanish had finally been driven to yield those parts of the coastline which they had stolen from the English years earlier when they had errowiusly claimed everything from Cape Horn to the Northlands. Finally, the obvious justice of the treaty would be the law for all men; the fur trade, British by right, would no longer be disputed by the conniving Spaniards. Now that the Spanish realized that England would gladly go to war to regain its lands, the cowardly King of Spain had finally ceded to the might of the British crown. A smile spread across Chip's dirty face as pride got the best of him. He had been looking for an opportunity to ask the captain if he could bring tea during tomorrow's meeting, just so he could be near the action. He didn't really hold any hope for his being allowed to do so. He imagined himself in Captain Vancouver's shoes; as commander of the Discovery with one hundred men at his command, he would sail to the farthest reaches of the globe under the proudly flown Union Jack. When he became a captain he would be a mighty explorer, carrying the power of the King to the furthest reaches of the globe, he would find the Northwest Passage. The captain before him had been so rash as to decide that the fabled passage did not exist, but Chip never doubted that he would succeed on his very first voyage. He would start by heading North to...

"Chip!"

"Y-yes sir!"

"Do you understand your commission?"

"Yes sir! I will go immediately sir!"

"And be smart about it. Quadra is a fine man, do not embarrass the King!"

"Yes sir!"

Captain Vancouver shook his head and returned to his work after pointing to the sealed paper on the corner of the desk. Chip slipped the sealed message into his pocket, leaving as silently as he had entered while the Captain flipped through a stack of rough charts on the cabin floor. Once the door was shut, Vancouver straightened and stared after his cabin boy. The captain had once been young, and it pained him to stifle the child's energy, but it was the commander's duty to preserve order. Without order, without every man knowing his place, without obedience and decorum, there was nothing.

Nothing.

Rowing towards his destination, Chip smirked with pride at how much smaller the Spanish ship was than the Discovery and his parted lips flashed his chipped tooth from which his nickname was taken. He served the mightiest King on Earth, the rightful leader of colonies the world over, of this he was certain.

Certain.

Having sent the invitation to the foreign captain who had been standing on deck when Chip came up alongside, the cabin boy prepared to pull away. Chip was rather disappointed that the sailors from Quadra's boat weren't as ugly as the harsh late-night talk aboard the Discovery had led him to believe they would be, but after hearing their atrociously funny language, his sense of superiority had returned. English was clearly reserved for only the most civilized.

Splash! Chip's absentmindedness had caused him to drop an oar overboard as he was busy slotting the other into the oarlock. He reached over the gunwale swiftly, and drawing from the experience of having reached too far over the side of his little rowboat as a young boy which had sent him for a swim on a lake back home, he retrieved the oar without upsetting the craft. Thank God the oar hadn't been out of reach; had it been, he would have needed to engage in an awkward pursuit by stationing himself in the bow of his dory and paddling it like a primitive Indian in a canoe. No, that would have been too humiliating, and to think that the Spanish might have seen it! He had been lucky, the high gunwale of the Spanish ship had hidden his antics from view; how debasing it would have been for the cabin boy of the great Captain Vancouver to be seen chasing an oar clumsily dumped overboard, as if he were one of the local barbarians!

The oars in place, Chip began rowing purposefully back toward the Discovery at full speed. The Spanish cast a casual glance at him as he increased his speed and the distance between them with every stroke. Rowing fervently to impress the uninterested onlookers and to compensate for his near embarrassment, Chip caught his starboard oar on the anchor rode of one of the other eleven European vessels moored in the cove. Cursing as he sought to realign his little boat towards the Discovery, he cast his eyes towards the still receding Spanish boat, and was relieved to observe that it had swung on its anchor, hiding him from the view of its occupants. His eyes made a quick 360° sweep to ensure that no one had seen his second inadequacy. He was about to set back to his travel when there was a rustling in a clump of bushes on shore and a native child of no more than nine years ran from her hiding spot and disappeared once more from view. Furious at himself for having been observed, and especially that this sign of weakness was observed by one of the natives who impetuously refused to surrender their land to the authority of his king, Chip uttered under his breath one of the many racist phrases he had learned from the hardened sailors, vowed to make a point of humiliating the next Indian he saw, and returned to his ship.

***

The Captain was furious. The lookout had reported Chip's incompetent rowing, and Vancouver had ordered Chip to be denied two meals, and to clean the companionway immediately. "Embarrassing every Englishman is direct disobedience to clear orders to maintain decorum," Vancouver had said, each word a piercing dagger to Chip's fragile self-respect. "Hey Chip! Be careful when you're cleaning the steps" one of the sailors had jibed, "if you get too much mud on you, your skin'll look Indian!" How Chip hated him. Purple with humiliation, he swallowed hard and kept scrubbing the mud of countless boots' passage over the steps. Back and forth he ground the cloth into the rutted wood, rhythmically, as if to the metre of a conductor's wand. His vision narrowed as he concentrated on his labour until he could only see his hands. He would have loved to dump the pail of harsh soap and mud onto the scoffing man, and he might have done just that had another sailor not walked by and bumped into the pail, sending the filth slopping over the floor, surging around Chip's red knees and kneading hands like a tidal wave. The mess and his degradation was one thing, but as the two men laughed gruffly at his mortifying predicament, a tide of red seethed through the cabin boy, and he rushed at the two. Striking with fists and teeth, Chip brought forth a hateful, guttural scream like the one he had voiced when slashed by the factory blades those five years previous. Within moments, however, the first man had knocked him down with a brutish clout to the head. The boots of the other dug into him as he writhed on the floor...

He awoke with a start in his bed, a barely audible whimper went up from his lips as he reached a hand down to feel his ribs where his last memory told him the worst hurt was. He winced at the pain, but as he ran his blood crusted fingers over his body, he was relieved to find no deep gashes or broken bones. He flopped backward onto his makeshift pillow and looked up towards the ceiling of his room. With puzzlement, Chip observed the porthole above his head. He was certain that the glass had vibrated presently, as if shivering from the cold outside. He stared at it for some moments, but it was still. There it was again! Just as before, the porthole quivered for a half second, then ceased. Many times this peculiar situation repeated itself; overcome with curiosity, Chip sat up in his bunk.

The land was ablaze! A great arrowhead of fire, blinding his night-vision, reached upwards into the black sky; orange claws of flame stretched upwards until extinguished by the cold night. As his sight cleared, Chip began to see black shapes moving about the great flare. Surely it was the Indians who had stupidly let a fire burn out of control; this would certainly be typical of the savages, Chip decided. They must be trying to put it out. The next day there would be a merry laugh around the breakfast table in the galley about how the Indians had lost control of their fire. Chip smirked to himself. He was about to leave his window to return to his slumber, but something about the way the subjects of his vision were moving about the glaring pillar held his eyes fast. After a minute, suspicion had become certainty, the Indians were not fighting the flames after all but were engaged in some sort of ceremony; surely it was a pagan human sacrifice in which they would drink the offering's blood – the men on the ship had graphically described the detestable practices of these savages!

And yet, there was an order to this madness which did not seem of the devil. It was a sort of dance in fact. Chip was intrigued. Opening the porthole a crack, Chip understood the cause of the portal's tremors, for a deep, resonant drum beat became audible to him now. He closed the porthole again to avoid the risk of waking up anyone else in his quarters, and laid his head back down on his pillow ponderously. Closing his eyes, he imagined men jumping and moving around this great fire, the largest he had ever seen.

In a minute his mind was made up. Chip, already dressed in his only clothes, slid softly off his bunk, put on his shoes, strung his pocket-knife around his neck, and slipped out the door. He did not worry about making too much noise down the first corridor, but once he arrived at the gangway up to the deck, he reverted to the manner of movement he had assumed in London after his accident when he was cast out by the factory owner. At that time, he had picked pockets to stay alive. Moving silently, touching only those boards which ten thousand trips up and down the companionway had taught him would not creak, he crept upwards inches at a time. The Captain's quarters was now immediately to his right. He could see the light streaming through every crack in and around the door. Vancouver was still at work on his charts, Chip presumed. He moved past the door and appeared on deck. An unexpected shuffling sound behind him caused him to drop deftly to the deck. Turning his head slowly to look behind, Chip saw the man on watch looking intently in his direction. Chip thanked heaven that he was hidden from the moonlight by the mast's shadow, the path which he had instinctively followed after so many months of shadow-living in befouled London alleys. The sentry, evidently satisfied, turned his back to Chip and returned to his stargazing and humming of some familiar English tune. Having learned his lesson, Chip completed his journey towards the dory on all fours, in the form and manner of a cat sneaking up on an unsuspecting bird.

Chip pushed off by hand to avoid any clanking and rowed a few tentative strokes to put distance between himself and the sentry, keeping the bulk of the Discovery between his dory and the mother ship. Soon he was just another insignificant shadow lost in the sea of shadows cast by the hulking vessels at anchor. The slow, steady swinging of these eleven envoys from the world's powers inscribed circles in their own slow time on the face of the glassy water, tethered to iron anchors biting into the floor of Friendly Cove. Slipping between obstacles in his path like a shark cutting silently through the water towards the smell of warm blood, Chip's roundabout path brought him steadily toward the radiating fire and beating drum. Always wary not to alert any watchmen on other ships, Chip would stop his rowing and coast past the looming wooden boats, oars just clearing the water. For these long seconds, the only audible sound was the gentle rippling of the dory's bow as it clipped through the water. When he lost speed, he synchronized his movements with the drum beat, letting the deep sound mask the squeaking of his oars; like a galley slave, Chip took four beats to bring his oars through one full motion. Each time his vessel began moving nicely again, Chip's body became still, undetectable, camouflaged in blackness and drums.

Docking amongst a jumble of driftwood, piled high by incomprehensibly powerful winter storms, he made fast the boat and stepped ashore. Chip brought himself slowly to the same bush from which he had been observed earlier that day, and peered cautiously through a perfectly situated hole at the ritual taking place for no observer but him. There was a great number of figures around the fire, a hundred at least. Most of them were nearly naked, and each was a beacon of light as the fire's illumination reflected from their glistening bodies, slick from the sweat caused by the dual stress of heat and motion. A group of women were beating brown drums. Each perfectly timed beat seemed to impart energy to the furiously dancing men to make one more jump, one more twirl, one more purposeful step. The rhythm was incessant, and the voices which joined it seemed equally determined to go on without end. Passionate, deafening, dynamic, the song and dance appeared more organic and natural than any entertainment affair he had ever seen.

Horror! Something touched Chip's shoulder. He whirled around, eyes wide, fists ready. Even before the hair had settled upon his head, he recognized what had startled him. It was a native boy, at least four years his elder, who was as apprehensive of Chip's reaction as Chip had been of the hand on his shoulder. For interminable seconds the two stared at each other, Chip's fists shaking, the boy's spear pointed with calm resolve in response. Chip's mind was devoid of anything but his own fear, and the even more present need to frighten his adversary into backing off. Nearly melting from fright, Chip held his stance, doing his best to appear absolutely confident despite the memory of factory blades slicing into his leg which was conjured up by the sharp blade aimed squarely at his chest. Then, without cause, the Indian lowered the point and walked past Chip, taking the cabin boy's wrist in his hand. Chip pulled away, furious that the savage should touch him. The other shrugged, made a motion with his head for Chip to follow, and began walking toward the fire. Confused and frightened, Chip whirled around and looked for his boat, but it was out of sight. Did he dare make a run for it? The sailors of his ship told stories of Indians who were brilliant killers with spears. He had been told that they could fell a deer at thirty paces with one throw. Chip could never get that far before the savage would be in pursuit, and even if he did get to his boat, he would be a sitting duck. Fleeing into the bushes was no better, for he had also heard tales of bears and wolves in these forests which took pleasure in rending men limb from limb. Chip's decision to follow the boy was simplified greatly by an impatient backward glance from his discoverer. Chip scurried to catch up, and followed a few paces behind.

With fear and trepidation, Chip trailed his captor into the ring of Indians, brightly illuminated by the blazing inferno. Upon seeing him, the ensemble fell absolutely silent. The boy with the spear spoke hurriedly in a tongue even more ridiculous than Spanish to an old man seated in a makeshift chair. Chip wondered how the old man could keep his eyes open, so heavy they looked with layers upon layers of wrinkles which rippled up his forehead. Forcing himself to consider more important things, Chip's knees softened, "They're deciding whether or not to sacrifice me!" How could he act to make himself less appealing to them? Act crazy? Sophisticated? Like one of his captors? Somehow pretend that he was a spirit? How could he make himself unacceptable to the ceremony? What pagan god were they going to sacrifice him to? The decision of how to act was answered by the old man's response, as indecipherable as the boy's question had been, and his sweeping gesture towards Chip. "They're going to cut my head off!" Chip's throat constricted as his eyes grew. In a moment the drums began again. Chip's captor approached him smiling, but the white boy saw no friendship in it. That haunting smile of mottled and missing teeth made Chip draw back in terror. Uttering some unknowable phrase in his alien language, the boy began pulling Chip towards the fire. Deep, ferocious, primal fear surfaced in decisive response. Chip snarled, pulled back and searched frantically in the ring of men and women who had returned to their chanting for a weakness through which he could escape, some crack through which he could disappear. Some eyed him, others looked towards the dancing men and the fire, but all were hostile, all were joining in the ritual of his death. They intended to savagely burn him to his bones in honour of their pagan lusts. He unclasped his knife and turned it menacingly towards the boy, who had taken on a distinctly reddish tint from the fire, accenting the devil within him.

Then there was laughter. Beginning with the boy, then growing into a wave of amusement which swept across the circle of bodies, guttural guffaws spread through the natives as they observed this funny white man who first tried to approach, but now searched in vain for a means of escape. The drums continued despite the interruption, however, and the voices picked up again. Chip was appalled at how they found his resistance to be not only paltry opposition, but even laughable! Then, to his great surprise, the boy who had found him passed Chip his spear by the handle. The boy's never-fading smile grew as he observed Chip's astonished expression. Once relieved of his burden, the boy joined in the dance, clearly inviting Chip to follow him. Absolutely confused, Chip looked down at his tiny pocket-knife clenched in a white and shaking hand, at the native spear in the other, and finally back at the boy who disappeared from view behind the fire in the circle of dancers proceeding ever around the flames.

As the boy began his second trip around the circle, he tugged at Chip's wrist once more. This time, he ceded to the Indian. Chip dropped the spear to the ground, re-clasped his knife and fused into the circle of dancers. He began walking around the circle in time, and the chorus of voices seemed to get louder in honour of his assention to the dance. Chip glanced apprehensively around, his captor boy was in front of him, and a muscular man followed behind; both of them processed in a different series of movements, but both sequences seemed absolutely appropriate. Chip's eyes turned to the open-mouthed faces around the perimeter, and as he did so, the people changed before his eyes. No longer were these a throng of murderous demons; rather there were strange, frightening people, but people nonetheless. Chip's awkward stumbling was still rather embarrassing, and the boy, whom Chip decided to call Long-Hair after the strong, black strands which descended much of his back, took pity on him. Taking hold of Chip's yielding wrists, the two of them began moving together; like a wounded animal whose health improved with each round of the circle, they picked up speed and purpose with each revolution. As Chip travelled along the inside of the ring, he became aware of the totality of the experience. Every person present was participating as fully as possible. Everyone partook in the chorus,whether mothers with nursing infants, little children, young warriors, or elders. There was no rule about who could participate, it was nothing like dances back home where only the rich could attend. Those without drums had something else in their hands, sticks to contribute to the beat, a hide which they were scraping, or some food which they were preparing. The old man was unique, for he had in his hand a piece of wood which he whittled furiously. Shavings flew from his work just like from Steven's planer, the great heap of spent wood ever growing at his feet, and the old man's forehead seemed even more wrinkled than previously, so intent was he upon his work. After some minutes of moving together with Chip's eyes absorbing the incredible sight with each passage, Long-Hair released his charge's arms. The boy returned to his unrestrained movement, leaving Chip to discover what remained of the dance for himself.

Still self-conscious of his artificial manner, Chip's brow furrowed as he strove to acquire the secret which he had not yet found. He was aware that his steps were unnatural, almost wooden in their stiffness, both because of his bad leg and from feeling detached from the music. Copying Long-Hair's movements, Chip found himself constantly tripping over his own feet and becoming frustrated; it was as if his pants were so starched that they restrained him, so rigid was his body. Chip's thoughts turned to his first few days at the factory when he was learning to operate the great machine. He had listened excitedly to the foreman, memorizing every procedure he was shown, and during his first hours working alone he had always recited the steps as he performed them with precision and rhythm. Some days later, when his production nearly doubled, Chip realized that he was no longer conscious of his actions; they had become second nature, just like walking. He became frightened, and resolved to start reciting his instructions once more lest he should forget an essential step. His dexterity dropped immediately as his mind began meddling with his body, and it was that day that he had nearly lost his life to the machine. *Don't think, just do.* Don't think, just do. Purposely surrendering his mind, Chip allowed his body to be governed not by his head, but by the beat. Closing his eyes, he ceased copying Long-Hair and began to create his own steps. At first walking straight ahead, Chip feared that he could not find the inspiration within himself to dance like the Indians, but each time he gave in to the urge to turn or leap, he strengthened his obedience to the dance. Emancipated from his brain, liberated from the need to conform, Chip's movements became progressively more lucid. Freed from the cruel master of thought, Chip dove into the dance, immersing himself in sense and movement.

Whirling around, touching the ground only briefly between jumps or bold steps, Chip felt his reason and thought liquefy and run out of him as the sweat began to pour down his face. Then, without knowing exactly why, he ripped the tattered shirt from his chest and thrust it into the fire. The Indian voices went up another level in approval of his show of commitment, driving him further down the path to kinaesthetic oblivion. Faces, fire, shoulders, feet, black night, pinpoint stars, looming trees, everything began to run together as Chip ceased to look about him. He was now one with the fire, one with the twenty men progressing in perpetual motion about it, one with the seventy voices which rang out in vitality, giving impetus to each movement, giving purpose to every footprint pounded into the beaten earth, giving wings to his deepest desire for elemental expression of passion which had been denied to him and to many since birth. For the first time, there was no King, no Country, no Ship, no Factory; even the pain from his lacerated leg and bruised ribs failed to touch his conscience. There was only intoxicating heat, the assault of sound upon his brain, the onslaught of earth and sky and fatigue on his muscles and the elemental demand that he continue in his trance which superseded all calls from his failing body to cease the madness. His heart was beating quickly now, powerfully, it was throbbing within him as if determined to not be outdone; it pumped as furiously as the drums, as repetitively as his legs and hands as they stretched to the highest heaven of humanity. Deep, strong, the drums were also making themselves felt inside his chest, and it was then that he realized, he felt not two heart beats, but one. The drum and his organ were in perfect time, everything was in perfect harmony. Everything was working together. The combined energy of stretched and beaten animal skins and his own blood gave him even more strength; real or imagined, it did not matter. With feral release, Chip loosed a cry such as he had never uttered. Urgent, driving, satisfying, he let it come forth again, in time with the native singers. Without thinking he let it surface yet again, goosebumps washing over him in tides of ecstasy. He opened his eyes widely again to the spinning world of bright light, glistening bodies, beating drums, looming sky, and seeing the open mouths of the indefatigable Indians, he understood that he was making the same sounds, he was singing the primal melody as confidently as any there. Abandoning whatever means of self-restrant he had learned from education or experience, Chip once again allowed the weight of his eyelids to plunge him into the black world of heightened sensation as he pumped his legs harder, shouted louder, twirled faster, becoming wholly animal, wholly human...

His head was bobbing with the drums even before he awakened some minutes after having collapsed from fatigue. He remembered the feeling of falling to the welcome earth below after one particularly high jump. He had been unafraid, welcoming whatever came. Propping himself up into a half-sitting position, Chip turned his attention from the still proceeding dance to the old man seated beside him. Whittling furiously, the wrinkled elder was so concentrated upon his work that he did not notice Chip until the cabin boy leaned his head over the old man's arm to observe what shape the wood was taking. Distinctly formed, the man was inscribing something into a paddle. After a few seconds, Chip realized that the man's masterful hands, guiding the whalebone blade in natural paths up and down the oar's length, were forming the image of tongues of fire upon the paddle's face. Within a minute, the old man held his work at arm's length and grunted in satisfaction. The old man then took a newly carved pendant which bore the same inscription as the paddle in his hand, and turning to Chip, placed the pendant around Chip's neck and the paddle in his hand. Chip took the paddle in his now steady hands, inspected it, nodded, and held it back out to the whittler. Clearly confused, the old man looked from Chip's face to the paddle and back again, he gestured towards the ring of dancers, and then at Chip, who needed no persuasion. Surprised by this gift, but understanding that it was a show of appreciation for having shared in their strange communion, Chip rose and returned to the dance with the paddle grasped tightly in his two hands. Following the path of his dance, up and down, twirling, coming to rest for a beat as every muscle in Chip's body tensed in anticipation of the next leap, the paddle became an extension of Chip's expression of humanity. The fire glinted spectacularly off the newly carved grooves, transferring the character of the fire to the paddle, his Blazing Paddle. The necklace danced about his bare neck, falling repeatedly upon his chest, producing a point of pain which reminded him of the wondrous emblem he wore. Complemented by the symbolic objects of his intensity, Chip renewed his resolve as he plunged ever deeper into the primal release of the perpetual dance.

***

"Chip!" The voice was Steven's.

"Chip! Get yourself out of bed! The captain's going to be expecting you at his quarters any minute now!" Steven shut the door and hurried off, shaking his head. He couldn't afford to help Chip get ready in time, the first mate would be making his rounds any minute and he was supposed to be on deck already.

Opening his eyes, Chip's brain was overcome with light, a bright morning light which streamed through the glass porthole into his room. The porthole was exactly as he had seen it before falling asleep following his nightmare, or had everything been a nightmare?

It was all gone. Chip nearly choked in rage as he realized that this glorious reality he had known so truly was nothing but a dream. Sneaking out, Long-Hair, the spear, the fire, the old man, drums, dancers, returning to the Discovery at the break of dawn, all a dream.

Numb from resentment towards the powers which should allow him this glimpse of heaven only to steal it away, Chip slunk out of bed. Surprised by the extreme stiffness of his leg, Chip recalled the beating he had received the night before, put on his shoes gingerly, and cast about for his shirt. Not finding it, he began searching frantically; he had already been late the previous day, and the captain would not deal leniently with repeated tardiness.

Chip kneeled down on the floor, and bent his head down to peer under his bunk in case the shirt had found its way there. A faint clunk got his attention, and he glanced down toward the sound's origin. There,

Nootka Nirvana

on the floor and hanging by a cord around his neck, was a pendant of a blazing paddle. With trembling fingers and stopped breath, Chip reached his right hand slowly to the floor and picked it up. The pendant did not disappear. Elated beyond measure, Chip thrust it under his pillow, and after choosing his roommate Jim's extra shirt to be his for the day, he donned it and rushed out of the room to Captain Vancouver's quarters. Reaching the companionway, Chip grasped the handle of the captain's door and took a moment to calm himself before entering. Ever since they had anchored in the cove many days ago, excitement had been building up inside him for this day when the treaty negotiations would occur, for this day when Spain would relinquish the coast. To his great surprise, Chip could not find that excitement within him; it was as if the anticipation had been drained from his blood the night before. Chip's eyes emerged from his puzzled expression and slowly refocused on the discovery's deck. Worn, dirtied boards made up the steps and companionway. Stabbing upward from the deck was a straight mast, tall and sterile. Staring past the uninteresting member to the sky behind which stretched to infinity, Chip remembered how it had appeared the night before, a saturated black accented by points of light in which he had lost, and found himself.

Souvenirs

Allison Trumble

The look in the Indian girl's eyes as she knelt before him, begging for food, was enough to make anyone give in. His own hunger forgotten, Colin gave her a large portion of the dried salmon that he had set aside for his own supper. She took it from his hands, and chewed it ravenously. She looked up at him again, licking her fingers, and said, "Thank you," before she scampered away. Colin was surprised, he hadn't known she spoke English. He shook himself out of his odd state of mind. He had always refrained from giving food to the Indians. They gambled away their ammunition and ate the salmon they were given to bait their traps. He didn't think that they deserved extra charity. He also knew that should he give them anything, they would just keep coming back for more, like a stray dog given a piece of meat. But there had been something in the way she looked up at him, with eyes that penetrated his, and he simply couldn't resist.

Colin Roberts had come to New Caledonia in the previous spring, on a ship that had come to collect furs from Fort Langley. He had been restless and unhappy in his monotonous upper-class English life, so he left his wife and home in London to fulfill his need for an adventure, a change of pace. He assured his wife that he would be back soon, that he would be away for only a few months. She would barely notice his absence, she was so wrapped up in her world of gossip and new fur coats. After staying at Fort Langley for a month or two, Colin had come up the river to Fort McLeod, where a flood had destroyed the entire fort. He helped to rebuild it over the summer, and then stayed on for the winter. The months that had passed since he had left London felt like an entire lifetime. The world across the Atlantic seemed no more than a strange dream, only staying in his mind because of its sheer absurdity. Here was a world that was fresh and real, more pure than anything he had ever lived. It was rustic and even crude. Rather than the stone that was the main construction material in London, everything here was made of wood. The only stone to be seen here was either on the rocky beach of the lake or in the hills surrounding it. Every task that he performed here had a direct and relevant result on his life. If he chopped firewood during the day, it fueled the fire that kept him warm that night. This kind of immediate link between his work and his life made him feel more fulfilled than he had ever been in England.

He saw the girl again the next day as she hauled snow indoors on a sled, where she would melt and heat it in kettles, then wash laundry with it. Her long hair fell in braids over her shoulders and down to her hips. Colin noticed that her hands as they gripped the rope of the sled were a shade lighter than the other Indians', as was her hair, meaning that she was most likely a half-breed. Colin guessed that her father had probably been one of the many white men who had passed through the fort. Judging by her age of about twenty or so, it could have even been someone from Simon Fraser's crew when he first established the fort in 1805.

The entire fort was awaiting the arrival of a hunting party that had gone out to bring back fresh meat. Everyone prayed that they would bring enough to feed them, but the last two hunts had brought back no more than a couple of rabbits and a fox. As Colin turned from the lake back to the fort, he could see that the girl was approaching him again. Fear of weakness turned to rage, and as she knelt before him, eyes sunken into their sockets with hunger, begging to him, he slapped her across the face with all the fury inside of him. His frustration in himself for giving her anything in the first place and his fear of it happening again brought the back of his hand flat across her left cheekbone. She fell to her side, giving him a look full of hurt and sorrow, before she got up and ran away. Colin seethed with anger; she wasn't just an Indian, she was a half-breed. From the way the other Indians treated her, he knew that they didn't respect her either. How could he have given her charity? When he saw her later as she sat turning the flexible white roots of the spruce into rope and cord, his disgust for her increased. He would turn his back, not wanting to look upon such a creature. But there was kernel of doubt in the back of his mind.

A few days later, Colin saw the girl coming toward him again. He was instantly angered and started to turn away, but she was offering him something. As she reached where he was standing, she opened her hands to reveal a stunning beaded necklace. She stretched up to put it around his neck, but he resisted her effort and took it in his hand.

"Thank you," he said gruffly. She seemed unsatisfied as she looked up at him, but she gave him a soft smile anyway before she turned away. Colin looked down to where the beads lay in his hand; they were glass, and of fine quality. Such things were rare in this part of the world, and as Colin realized their value, he suddenly became very ashamed. She must have traded many of her belongings for those beads, and he had been angry with himself for giving her a piece of fish. Though he wasn't one to wear jewelry, he fastened the string of beads around his neck. He looked up to the girl who was walking away, and he watched her with fresh, untainted eyes. His contempt for her gone, he could see that she was quite beautiful, unique in looks due to her mixed heritage. She was tall and slender, and walked with a grace and confidence that wasn't snobbish, but honest. She was young, but not too young to be considered romantically, he guessed about seventeen. As though his thoughts were being read, an image of Colin's wife came into his mind. He almost laughed at the striking contrast between the two women. Mrs. James spent her days ordering the servants about and gossiping over tea; she never seemed to cease talking. Despite his year-long absence, her loud, nasally voice resonated through Colin's head, as he gazed after a girl who had spoken no more than a few short words to him.

One day the young Indian woman sat indoors, building a canoe from birch bark. She sewed the sheets of bark together with spruce roots and shaped the curving prow that would glide lightly over waves and hold firm through rushing currents. Colin entered the room and walked towards her. When he neared, she must have read his face, or perhaps just knew the ways of people enough to guess what his purpose was. She rose and spoke to him, "Don't worry, you're forgiven. I'm Isabelle." She extended her hand the way the men did, strong and sturdy.

"I'm Colin," he replied as he shook the hand that did everything from build canoes to wash laundry and prepare food.

"I must work now. May I speak with you later?" Colin nodded and with that, she turned and continued with her task, her nimble fingers darting in and out with the bone needle.

As the days progressed, Colin and Isabelle would often take walks in the thick woods where the snow wasn't deep. There was little to do around the fort during the winter months, and they would both slip away from their respective communities, unnoticed. They shared stories of their lives, and marveled at the differences in the paths traveled.

Colin learned that Isabelle's mother had died when she was only six years old, and that she did not even know her father's name. She explained how her mother's sister had cared for her, but had frowned upon her mother's activities with the white men, and therefore frowned upon Isabelle. She had never really found acceptance, and had developed an independent nature. Colin tried to explain life in London and how his proud and overbearing mother had eventually prodded him to marry someone much the same. Isabelle found the unspoken rules and expectations of social life in England hard to understand; the silent backstabbing that went on among friends and family was completely foreign to her. She also tried to imagine the city, and longed to see it, having known only the woods and the fort her whole life.

Colin lay in bed, savouring the endearing qualities that Isabelle possessed. She was honest and direct, uninhibited by the proper etiquette that the women Colin had known in England were trained in from birth. She was naive, yet she had a certain wisdom about her, a way of seeing the truth of a matter, despite the fog that might surround it. Colin was suddenly interrupted from his reveries by a sound at the door of his sleeping quarters. He looked up to see Isabelle standing in the doorway. She entered the room made of logs and began to remove her clothes. Colin thought this a rather bold and somewhat crass move, but he wasn't going to complain, as he was overwhelmingly drawn to her. As she climbed under the furs that covered his bed, Colin was thankful that as one of the few English gentlemen at the fort, he had a private room in which to sleep. When Colin awoke, she was already gone, but the bed was still warm where she had lain.

Weeks passed, and the two often met at night in addition to their daily sojourns. As the days got longer and the weather got warmer, they were both busy with tasks around the fort during the daylight hours, but they were still able to share the nights.

One sunny afternoon when the snow was high in the mountains and no longer in the fort, three canoes came across the lake to the fort, where they would rest for the night. They were carrying furs to Fort Langley, which would then be shipped to England. One of the men had broken his arm and they needed someone from the fort to replace him. Colin could not imagine leaving Fort McLeod, leaving Isabelle. He most certainly could not imagine going back to England, to his wife, after living so simply and so happily here.

Isabelle found Colin sitting on a log. He was taking a break from felling trees to be used for construction and firewood. She had a glow about her and a glint in her eyes. He smiled at her and she spoke to him calmly,

"I'm carrying a child, Colin. You're going to be a father."

Colin was shocked into speechlessness. He hadn't planned for this to happen, he didn't know what to do. He didn't want to be a father, not in this place. He wasn't ready to make that kind of a commitment or to settle down in this remote land. His wife in London was expecting him home, she thought that he'd only be gone a few months. How could this be happening, what could he do? He left her side and returned to his work, chopping into the trunks ceaselessly, trying to forget the news that he had just heard. Eventually his body was exhausted and he did the only thing he could think of. Fingering the beads at his neck, he found the Captain of the canoes and told him, I'll go with you.

"Great, I was worried we wouldn't find anyone. We leave at daybreak," was the terse reply.

Colin stood on the deck of the ship, watching as the British coast came more into view. He would be back in London soon; home, he supposed he could call it. As it got closer it became more and more desirable, and the life that he had left over the ocean dissolved into a dream. The only thing remaining to ensure its reality were the beads hanging around his neck.

Journey of Survival

Katie Maximick

Isaac Harrison wearily entered the secluded log cabin on a chilly September evening. He hung his coat on the nail next to the door, and strolled into the kitchen where his family patiently waited for him at the already set table. Three children and a wife were what Isaac loved to come home to, and there they sat grinning up at their loved father and husband with big, anticipating eyes. His oldest daughter, Belinda, sat on one side of the table with her hands neatly folded in front of her on the table; Dora, his seven year old daughter, sat eagerly across from her elder sister with her two year old little brother, Toby, next to her. At one end sat his wife, Margaret. After being married to her almost seventeen years, his heart still skipped a beat whenever he looked upon her beautiful face.

He took his seat at the table and smiled at Margaret flirtatiously, causing her to blush deeply. As he turned and looked at his lovely daughter, Isaac couldn't help but feel a miserable pain deep inside his heart because of the news that he had to tell her. Nervously, he cleared his husky throat in preparation and gazed up at the young lady one more time.

"Bel," he began "there is an important matter that I need to discuss with you right now. Now, you and I both know that you just turned sixteen, and you are clearly becoming quite a young lady. When women reach your age, they have the tendency to run off and be married." Bel smiled, happily. How she adored her father.

"Oh, Papa!" she laughed. "How you do carry on! I won't run away and get married. You know me too well to assume that!" Margaret frowned and fumbled with the cloth napkin on her lap, knowing that Bel certainly was not going to like what Isaac was about to tell her.

"Exactly my point, Bel. If it were up to you, you'd never leave this house, but now that you're older you don't really have much of a choice . . . As you know, I was at the Fort today and I just happened to run into your Aunt May. I had quite the conversation with her about a suitor for you. Well, I have been keeping quite close contact with her lately about finding you a proper husband and we did just that." Bel's green eyes widened in horror, and her face grew a terrible white. The dark, silky brown hair around her forehead looked almost black next to her new facial color, and her beautiful face seemed to twist into a miserable one.

"Oh!'' she gasped under her breath. "But, Papa I-"

"No, Bel. Not this time. You're sixteen years old, and it's about time that you began to live your own life. There's no need for your mother and I to look after you anymore if you're able to look after yourself, right? We could be saving more money if you were living on your own . . ." The supper table became silent and all poor Bel could do was stare blankly ahead of her. Her chin began to tremble as tears started to fall from beneath her dark eyelashes.

"Oh, Papa! How could you?!" she cried, rising from the table, and with no response from her father, Bel ran into her bedroom flinging herself onto her bed sobbing. Moments later, she was joined by her mother, who in the presence of Isaac couldn't say any word of defense for her daughter. After all, it wasn't a woman's place.

Bel sat up, her face showing all signs of one that had been crying for quite a while. Margaret sat down beside Bel and placed a soft, plump hand on her daughter's back. Margaret was a pretty little creature, short, and fairly plump. What she was most prized for was her calm and soothing nature. Unlike her daughters and her husband, Margaret had golden blond hair (which was passed onto Toby) and a short figure. Isaac, Bel, and Dora were all quite tall for their age.

"Now, now, Bel," Margaret said soothingly. "Your father is only trying to do what's best for you, and what you need for your future. You know that he loves you dearly." Bel looked at her mother sadly, trying hard to believe her words.

"Do I, Mother?" she asked. "How could he possibly want what is best for me when he's deciding my entire future for me? I don't want to get married, not yet anyway. I want to stay here and watch Dora and Toby with you! Forcing me to leave and marry some old man that I've never met isn't what's best for me!" Bel's cheeks were hot in anger and frustration, and her green eyes now flickered in fury.

"Please, Bel. Lower your voice before your father hears you,"

Margaret ordered. Knowing well not to disobey her mother, Bel not only lowered her voice, but lowered her head as well, as if in defeat.

"I cannot do this, Mother," she gasped, beginning to sob again. "I'm not strong enough to leave my home. I can't just leave you and the children. I love you far too much to even think of doing that. Why would he want to do this?"

"Well, you are sixteen now. I was married when I was fourteen and it was also an arranged marriage. You see, Bel, that's just the way life goes, and as a woman you must follow that path so that you may lead a happy life, like I did with your father," Margaret explained, wiping a tear off of Bel's face. "Grasp this opportunity, Bel, and take charge of it while you can. This just might be the best thing that has ever happened to you." Bel sighed deeply and mournfully.

"I suppose I don't have much of a say in what happens from now on, then, do I?" she asked. Margaret shook her head. "Then all I can do is wait for my wedding day. When am I to be leaving here Mother?"

"In the spring, I think. Your father and I planned that you live with your Aunt May in Fort Langley until you get married; then life will take you away as it did me. Don't cry about it anymore, Bel. You can't stop it, but you can try to make the best out of it. Will you try for me, Bel? Please?" Margaret's blue eyes were so large and soft, that Bel couldn't let her down.

"Of course, Mother," she almost whispered, dropping her head down once again. This time it was surely in defeat. "I'll try."

***

"Aahh!!!" screamed Margaret one November afternoon. There she stood, high on her wooden table chair screaming at the top of her lungs. Annoyed with her mother's overly feminine frights, Bel stood below her, staring up with an irritated expression.

"Really, Mother. It was only a mouse. You should be used to them by now," Bel chastised, holding the broom that had chased the brown rodent back down the crack it had entered through.

"How am I supposed to get used to those horrid little monsters, creeping around as if they owned this house?!" she cried, descending from her sanctuary. "They just make the hair rise all over my body! Yuck! I wish your father had picked a more settled area than these woods, Bel. It would make life so much easier for all of us." Margaret was forced to stop her complaints to cough rather violently, which worried Bel.

"Mother," she began, trying to ignore that cough, "Papa chose these woods because they're absolutely crawling with animals for him to trap. In case you forget, Mother, he's a fur trapper!" teased Bel. Margaret looked at her daughter in surprise.

"Don't you try to remind me, Belinda-Lee Harrison! Here's something that I'll remind you. That butter needs to be churned. It can't form itself you know." Bel laughed, her golden voice ringing throughout the house. It was almost as if Bel had completely ignored the fact that she was to be leaving that little cabin in a few months, because Margaret never saw Bel cry once after that wretched evening. Bel continued to smile and laugh as she did previous to her father's decision, and nothing seemed ever to bother her or make her feel miserable as it had before.

"You're looking awfully tired today, Bel," Margaret pointed out, taking the broom out of her daughter's hands. "You're slow on your chores, and there are small bags under your eyes as if you hadn't had a wink of sleep."

"That's because I didn't," Bel confessed, biting her bottom lip. Margaret sighed in annoyance.

"Well, I suppose I'm not surprised. Nothing you do ever surprises me, but I'll be in my grave before that butter is made if you don't get on with it. And if it doesn't pain you to tell me, just why in Heaven didn't you get any sleep last night?" Margaret stood firmly.

"How could I have possibly fallen asleep last night? It was raining and blowing divinely all night long! I can just feel the winter coming upon us shortly! Snow is so wonderful, too! I can't wait to play in it! Oh, Mother, how can you not be excited?" asked Bel in disbelief of her mother's unimpressed expression.

"How? First of all, I hate the cold and you know that!" Margaret laughed. "Especially when that nasty wind blows my petticoats up around my face, that's why I hate the cold!" The two laughed merrily together in the kitchen as the other two children played foolishly around in leaves outside the house.

***

When the cold weather arrived and the ground was dusted with the white snow Bel loved so much, it was expected that she'd be happy; but she wasn't. The fact that she was to be leaving in only one month frightened her. She couldn't imagine the problem away anymore, as she had the previous months. No longer could Bel shake off the fact she was going to be married. No longer could she put on a smile and pretend all was well in the world. No. Bel was miserable to the core, and not even the laughter of her beloved siblings could make her smile.

Bel was looking forward to her departure as much as a stab in the back. She lumbered around the house silently, not speaking a word about Dora's new wooden animals or Toby's wonderful snow angels in the front yard, not even smiling to watch the brand new kitten struggle to chase a larger mouse. No, none of those things helped her much either. Margaret couldn't stand to see her daughter behaving in such a manner any longer, so she decided one day to say something about it.

"Bel, you simply must stop being so sad and unhappy all of the time." She finished with an especially bad sounding cough, the sound of which had begun to concern the entire family, not just Bel.

"Oh, Mother, you have to do something about that cough. It's sounding worse and worse all the time."

"Don't change the subject," Margaret said sharply.

"But Mother. I just can't be happy all of the time when my life's about to end in only a month. You don't understand what I'm going through!" she protested, sitting down in a nearby armchair.

"Oh, I don't, don't I?" she asked. "I already told you that I did the exact same thing as you, and I was younger. Drat this blasted cold!" Margaret sniffled and continued to feed the potbellied stove, which was beginning to glow a hot crimson red.

"But were you like me, Mother? Happy to be 'married' to my family rather than married to a man? My happiness was stolen from me that dark, September night, although I did not really know it at the time." Margaret looked at her daughter suspiciously.

"Why is it that you were happy and just fine before; but now you're rather depressed and miserable all the time?" she asked.

"You can't imagine your troubles away forever, Mother, like I've been trying for so long,'' Bel sighed, shaking her head sadly. Margaret threw her hands up in the air, helpless.

"You shouldn't allow that one decision to ruin the rest of your life, Bel. Your imagination and happiness shouldn't be burnt out, tossed away. If you must, strive harder and think of this as one of the many challenges that you must conquer in your life. Challenge your happiness." She finished by wiping her hands on her apron and kissing Bel on the forehead.

"Mother?" Bel asked before Margaret left the room. "I'll try, but I cannot promise anything."

That night at the supper table, Isaac – back from one of his many trips – smiled happily towards his daughter, a change from the concerned frown he usually had on every evening. Bel was quite suspicious about her father's happiness, so she decided to remain silent.

"Good news from your Aunt May, Bel," he began. Bel finished

swallowing and looked up at her father, nervously.

"What about?" she asked.

"She told me that your fiancé is quite excited about meeting you. Of course, I had to explain to your aunt what you looked like, but I'm pretty sure that he got the picture." A healthy blush filled Bel's cheeks; and before she could stop herself, she said:

"Did she say anything else about him?" That old twinkle filled her father's eyes and he laughed heartily. "I can see you're thirsting for knowledge, Bel!" He teased.

"Wel-l," he began slowly, purposely trying Bel's patience, "she said that he was of a decent, younger age – twenty-four, I believe – and supposedly he's quite the handsome man. Twenty-four isn't too young for you, is it?" he asked. Bel shook her head quickly, relieved that he wasn't over forty. Suddenly, Margaret drew her napkin to her mouth to muffle an extremely violent, painful sounding cough.

"Excuse me," she said meekly. Bel looked desperately towards her father. Her mother's cheeks looked unusually crimson for that time of year, and a few drops of sweat beaded her forehead.

"You aren't looking well, Margaret, and you haven't been for the last little while. I believe you're coming down with something," Isaac said, worried. Margaret mustered up a smile.

"Oh, no Isaac. It's only a small cold, and hardly anything to be concerned about. You too, Bel. I don't want both of you fussing over me as if I were a small child all of a sudden. I'll be alright." The family resumed eating once again, but there was an eerie silence hanging over them.

***

Margaret had underestimated her 'cold' severely. Two weeks later, it had become dreadfully worse so that Margaret couldn't even leave her bed. Isaac went on another expedition; this time it wasn't to trade furs, but to fetch the doctor from the fort for his wife. He had left in an awful hurry and even forgot to take his rifle. Isaac never forgot his rifle. Unfortunately, Isaac had been taking an extremely long time returning home with the doctor. After six hours, Bel became worried.

The snow was deep, and the nights bitter cold. Bel worked hard to keep the fire warm for her sick mother, hurrying to the dry shed outside in the yard. She'd bundle up in scarves and her paletote to face the freezing cold wind and to carry in wood by the armfuls to stack beside the little wood stove. Dora and Toby were far too young to help out their older sister, leaving poor Bel to cook, clean, take care of her mother, and mind the children all by herself. She had never done that before because Margaret had always been there with her to help her out with chores and guide her through her tasks, but her mother was of no use to her now.

Late into that night when the children were all asleep and the snow was falling steadily, Bel sat at her mother's bedside, kneeling on the floor with a basin of cold water. Margaret had lain in that bed many times before, not sick from fever, but ill from several miscarriages. Tenderly, Bel continued to dab Margaret's hot face with the cold cloth, trying to ease some of her mother's pain.

"I wish it were me instead of you," Bel whispered to her mother. "Then you wouldn't have to go through all of this." She was almost in tears. All of the stress of her ill mother, minding the children, and taking care of everything was far too much to put on Bel's shoulders all at once. She was tired, miserable, and, most of all despaired for the health of her mother.

"Bel?" Margaret asked a few moments later with a hoarse voice. Bel, happy to hear her mother speak, placed the cloth back into the basin quickly and sat up closer so that she could hear whatever Margaret had to say.

"Yes, Mother? I'm here," she responded, grasping her mother's hand in her own.

"Has-has your father returned with the doctor yet?" Bel looked sadly upon her mother.

"No, Mother. He hasn't come home yet. I'm not sure where he is or why he's taking so long, but don't fret, he'll be here shortly, you'll see," Bel coaxed. She was very badly off, and Bel knew it was true; she just didn't want to believe it.

"I'm going to die, Bel," she whispered. Bel shook her head.

"No, Mother. You're going to be back to your old self in no time. I don't know why you keep assuming that you're going to die! It's silly!" Bel chastised, trying to conceal her concern for her mother's health. Margaret smiled up at her daughter peacefully. Her golden hair sprawled around her face like an angel's would be; her cheeks red and hot like the stove, and her smile seemed to be the ray of sunlight in that stormy bedroom.

"I only wish the children could say good-bye, but they might catch the fever . . . Oh, and if only your father . . ." Tears swelled in Margaret's brown eyes as she thought of her beloved husband whom she couldn't kiss farewell. "I love you, Bel. You're my pride and joy, and I know that I can die peacefully because you have a safe and secure future." A knot formed in Bel's throat and a tear dropped onto her mother's hand.

"But Toby and Dora don't have a secure future, Mother, so you can't go!" she begged.

"I trust that you will ensure their future, Bel. I just wish that I could live to see yours." Bel shook her head in disbelief. Tears were now pouring down her cheeks.

"You will live to see mine!" she cried. "You will!" Margaret simply smiled once again and raised her arm to bring her daughter down to her for one last embrace. The hug was weak, but love shone through it like a warm summer's day.

"Good-bye, Bel."

"Good-bye . . ." Bel cried. Down, down came her mother's pale arm from Bel's neck, and without a sound, Margaret was gone. At first, Bel didn't know what to do. She stared down upon her lifeless mother in shock, with tears almost frozen on her cheeks just like her mother's heart. Then, with a sharp cry, Bel fainted.

"Bel? Bel, wake up!" cried a tiny, high voice. Bel opened her heavy eyelids to stare upon the small, round face of her little sister holding a candle in the darkness. She was confused, not knowing where she was, what had happened, or why she had fallen on the wooden floor. Then she saw her mother's white, stiff, and cold body lying on the low bed beside her.

"Quick, Dora!" she cried, jumping to her feet. "Get out before you catch the fever!"

"But, Momma!" Dora yelled, beginning to sob. Bel pushed Dora fiercely out of the morbid bedroom and out into the hallway, closing the door behind both of the daughters.

"She's gone, Dora." Bel's voice quivered with emotion, and tears streamed down her face.

"Where's Papa?" she asked. Bel shrugged. "Bel, what are we going to do?!" She clasped her hands over her mouth, frightened, as if to stop a murderous shriek from escaping her mouth.

"I don't know, Dora . . . Where's your brother?"

"Still sleeping."

"Go wake him up. We need to start packing so we can get out of here as fast as we can," Bel explained. She paused to rub her eyes tiredly; and when she saw that Dora hadn't moved, she looked up. "Hurry!" Unwillingly, little Toby was dragged out of his trundle bed and brought into the living room, where Bel was rushing around trying to gather items together.

"Wait!" cried Dora. Bel stopped searching the cupboard and stared at her little sister. "Where are we going, Bel?"

"To the Fort. We can stay with Aunt May, of course."

"But we don't know Aunt May! And we've never been to the Fort. How are we supposed to get there?" Dora asked, her hands on her little undeveloped hips.

"We'll walk."

"Walk? Bel, are you out of your mind? We'll freeze to death out there with no horses to help us!"

"Either you walk with us, or you stay here in this depressing home. It's up to you," Bel replied, rather coldly. Dora's chin quivered, and her eyes watered; and soon afterward, she fled the room to cry. It must have been difficult for Dora to go through, but Bel was taking the worst part for all of them, holding on bravely by a thin string. She explained what happened to Margaret to Toby, and he cried for a little while but soon fell asleep in the armchair while Bel packed a small bag.

The house was searched for necessities, but not much was to be found that was an absolute must. After Bel had cleverly sewn two separate strips of tough material onto a sac, she began to fill it with what the three would need for the journey. Bread, apple, preserves, cheese, and dried, salted beef were packed safely into the sak, wrapped with a warm, large blanket that they might need on the way.

Bel got the children dressed warmly in layers upon layers of clothing then quickly dressed herself as the children played outside the house for the last time. Bel threw on her mother's brown paletote because it was much warmer than her own and was ready to leave.

The morning sun hadn't yet risen, but the dawn was bright enough to allow them to see around the forest for a little while. As the family headed out of the house, Bel saw, in the corner of her eye, the rifle hanging above the door, and carefully strapped it over her shoulder. With the children, the sak, and the rifle, the family was all set to go to Fort Langley.

Bel closed the door behind them and sighed. She didn't want to leave their home, their mother . . . It was hard on the heart when she turned her back to that little log cabin, but Bel knew that it had to be done. She glanced ahead of them, as the sky grew brighter with morning. Those next steps into the deep snow were also the next steps into their future.

The tall evergreens were blanketed and weighed down with ice and snow; the forest floor was covered in drifts and bare spots, and the creeks were edged with transparent little sheets of ice. Bel normally would find this to be absolutely breathtaking, but she found it only to be an obstacle that she would have to overcome. Nature became foe, not friend.

After only a half an hour of walking, Toby wanted to walk by himself, and when Bel protested because he would slow them down terribly, Toby began to sob, making them stop all together. Irritated, Bel let the red cheeked little boy down from her arms and continued to trudge through the deep snow with Dora jumping behind in Bel's footprints.

The wagon tracks from her father's departure were no longer visible, but the path was still reasonably clear. The snow was falling softly, being of no bother to the group with its gentleness, and there was no wind to terrorize and chill them through their layers of clothing.

When it seemed as if they'd been walking for hours, it would end up to be only minutes. Dora would have to stop and rest once in a while, for she wasn't as strong as Bel, and her legs were much shorter. Toby continuously wanted to be placed down and picked back up again; although sometimes this was good because Bel's arms would need a break and she couldn't bear the pain of his body forcing the rifle into her hip any longer.

"How long have we been walking for?" asked an out of breath and hopping Dora from behind. Bel sighed and shifted Toby across to her other hip.

"I suppose around four hours. Why?"

"Because I'm dreadfully hungry." Bel stopped. She hadn't even thought once about the food that was in the sak! She glanced around them trying to find a dry area where they could sit; and when she saw the dry, snowless ground beneath a gigantic cedar tree, she almost ran to it.

The blanket was set down, and the bread and cheese was partially eaten by Toby and Dora, yet Bel didn't eat. She had lost her appetite a while back, so she split her rations between her siblings. Staring blankly towards a strange looking lump of snow, Bel thought of what was to become of them. She didn't know, and, frankly, it scared her that she wasn't sure. Anything could happen to them between that spot under the cedar tree and the Fort, and suddenly Bel became more aware of her surroundings as the children ate. The children ate as if they hadn't been fed in weeks, but Bel didn't have the energy to scold them on their manners. She remained staring ahead at that strange lump of snow as if in a trance until she packed up the remaining food and prepared to leave.

They were back on the road shortly; and after another hour or so, the trail they were following seemed to gradually become grown over with young saplings and fallen, rotting trees. Bel stopped in front of a log, confused and extremely panicked. She didn't know where she was! They must've somehow wandered off of the trail. Her breath floated in the air like the smoke from a chimney.

"What's the matter?" asked Dora. "Why does the trail end here?" Bel looked around feverishly. Where were they?

"Dammit!" she yelled, frightened, followed by an innocent gasp from Dora. 'Think, Bel, think', she told herself over and over, even closing her eyes to think of what she could do. Bel was so desperately tired and miserable that she found it extremely difficult to concentrate on anything. Dora still stared at Bel with wide eyes, and Toby gazed at her with a strange expression. "We're off the trail, Dora. It doesn't end here because we're not even on it to begin with. I don't know when or where we got off of it, but we're here aren't we?" Dora's frightened expression didn't help the situation much, but Bel glanced behind them with the only possible solution she could think of, even though it was a rather obvious one.

"W-what are we going to do, Bel?" asked her little sister who was almost brought to tears. Determined, Bel bit her lip and turned around, beginning to walk back the way that they had arrived.

"We'll follow our footsteps back until we get back onto the trail again. That's all we really can do."

"Down please, Bel," asked Toby. The snow wasn't very deep, so Bel placed him down and he jumped forward racing along the footsteps.

"No, Toby! Stay close by. Don't go running ahead," she warned, but it was as if he didn't hear her. Moments later he stopped rather abruptly.

"Look, Bel," he said pointing. "A cat." Bel looked around but she didn't see a cat anywhere.

"Toby, I don't see a-" a shrill scream interrupted Bel's words and she heard Dora fall to the ground behind her. She glanced behind her then looked towards Toby again and saw an extremely large cougar creeping towards her little brother. Her heart jumped and she screamed:

"Toby! Lay down, now!" Without question, Toby joined Dora and lay down in the snow. Bel pulled the loaded rifle off her back clumsily and glanced at the large cat once more. It was still moving in on Toby! Without hesitation, Bel bravely aimed the gun at the cougar, closing her eyes as she pulled the trigger. Bang! When she opened her eyes again, she saw the tail of the golden cat slip away quickly into the bush;

and it was gone. Of course, she didn't really expect to shoot the cat with her eyes closed, but it was gone none-the-less. Toby's head popped up, and Bel swept him up quickly into her arms, hushing his frightened soul. The gunshot had sent his heart beating rapidly, and his brown eyes seemed to be frozen in a very wide position.

"It's alright, Toby. The bad cat is gone now," Bel soothed. She carried Toby over to Dora's unconscious body and shook her awake. "Dora, wake up. The cougar's gone. Come on, get up! We have to go." The rifle was hung over her shoulder with her one free hand and Bel smiled to herself. She had successfully scared away a wild beast!

"Oh, Bel!" cried Dora as she dusted the snow off of her paletote. "I was so terribly frightened! I couldn't help but faint." They began to walk again.

"Oh, well . . . It sure is strange to see a cougar so far from the mountains this time of year. I didn't expect to come across one," Bel explained, glancing to where the cougar had disappeared.

"It's a good thing you brought Papa's gun, or we could've all been killed!" Dora exclaimed, growing scared of just the thought.

"Nah, I would've gotten a stick and either beat it with it if it came too close or scared it away." Dora looked at Bel in awe from behind

"You sure are brave," Dora breathed, smiling

"Well, Dora, I sort of have to be . . ."

They found the path half an hour later. Even though they had lost that amount of time, Bel couldn't help but feel relieved that they had some sort of guide to safety. No longer did she feel unsafe, but she took precautions for that missing cougar just the same.

As the afternoon rolled around, the snow became heavier; and the wind started to pick up. Bel wrapped her scarf around her mouth and pulled down her cap to cover her ears from the cold. She then picked up Toby in her arms and ordered Dora to hold onto her sak and not to let go, no matter what happened.

The wind and snow were almost blinding Bel completely, but this only pushed her to strive harder and to keep on going. Cold and scared, Toby dug his little face into the inside of Bel's paletote, and Dora hid behind so close that she couldn't feel the bitter wind upon her face. Bel's legs began to tire immensely. She was cold, exhausted, and even a little bit frightened. Snow whirled up around her like hissing snakes striking their deadly tails into her sore, red face. Clumps of snow would fall upon her from the swaying pines above and still the wind only seemed to blow harder and harder. Her eyes stung from straining through the whirling snow and her nose, well, she couldn't even feel her nose!

Bel was taking the brutal beating for all three of them; but she didn't mind so much, because she kept reminding herself that it was now her duty to see that the children would be safe. She'd go to any length to make sure they made it safely to Fort Langley. The gloves on her hands seemed as protective as paper in that wind, and her feet were as numb as ice. How could she go on? One would've given up long ago; but when Bel looked down at Toby and felt Dora clinging desperately onto her paletote, she couldn't help but feel pity for them. She would continue her trek without mumbling a word of complaint to the others. After all, they were all on the same boat.

Thoughts that kept her mind off of the freezing wind, her numb limbs, and her burning face raced through Bel's mind as they walked toward their destination. She imagined her fiancé: a young, handsome man whose smile could unlock any girl's heart, who had good manners and a wonderful personality. These were now her expectations after all of the praise Aunt May gave that young gentleman. But as the journey worsened, that young handsome man faded into an old, ugly, ill-mannered fur man who would take her away and give her fourteen children. Bel couldn't help but imagine that after a little while.

They had been traveling exhaustibly for at least eight hours, and Bel was growing incredibly concerned. The sky was darkening, and the clouds were thickening as they usually did around five o'clock in the winter; but this was different. They had no lantern, and there was no sight of the Fort yet. Without saying a word of her worries, Bel began to cry softly. Dora or Toby didn't hear her sniffles, but they felt her tenseness and for her sake, didn't say anything. She had basically given up. It was now dark, and there they trudged in the middle of the woods not knowing how far that they had to go. Salty tears began to freeze on her cheeks, but Bel didn't bother to wipe them away. She had no strength to spare.

"Did you hear that, Bel?" asked Dora from behind. Bel's heart jumped, thinking that once again, they were in danger.

"He-Hear what?"

"That noise. I can't quite describe it." They stopped so that they could all hear what Dora had heard. Bel strained her ears to listen, and suddenly, she heard muffled laughter. The laughter of a group of people. They must be near the Fort! Excitedly, Bel began to briskly jog down the path, using the last amount of energy she had to get there.

"Slow down, Bel! You're going much too fast!" Dora whined.

"No, Dora! Hurry! Don't you dare dawdle now!" she cried.

Soon the trail widened; and there through the darkness, they could see the outline of the Fort's high walls and lanterns spread around by guards. Grabbing Dora's hand, Bel pulled her towards the gate where they came across the guard.

"What are you doing out so late, ma'am?" asked the warmly dressed man. Bel was almost crying again, but this time in happiness

"Oh, sir. I beg of you to let us in. We've walked since dawn to come here and find my aunt," Bel explained, out of breath. The guard scratched his chin and looked at each of them.

"Well, what is your aunt's name?"

"May Harrison, the widow. Do you know of her?" she asked hopefully.

"Ah! Ms.Harrison. Why, I didn't think she had any other relations beside her son. Are these your children ma'am?"

"No, sir. They're my brother and sister. May we please come in now, sir? I do not believe my aching feet can stand anymore, and I believe that I am about to faint from exhaustion!" The guard chuckled merrily. It was nice to hear laughter again.

"Sure thing. Listen, if you want to know, your aunt lives in the third white house on your left as you walk in. Good-luck, miss." The gates were opened and Bel looked at the guard graciously.

"Sir, you have no idea how thankful I am for your generosity and kindness. Have a good night," she said, smiling. As Bel, Toby and Dora wandered into the fort, all three of them gazed around in awe. They had never seen such big buildings in such a small area before! It was all so new to them, but the cold and darkness seemed to ruin it for them. They needed to hurry to Aunt May's!

Finally they were there. It almost made that long, hard journey worth it . . . almost. Bel knocked on the third white house to the left, and it took a while for someone to come to the door. A snooty looking servant appeared and gazed out at the three strangers curiously.

"May I help you?" the man asked. Bel smiled.

"Is this the residence of May Harrison?" she asked.

"Yes, Miss, it is."

"Well, I am her great niece, Belinda Harrison. She was expecting me next month, but a terrible thing has happened, and I was forced to arrive dreadfully early," Bel said quickly. The servant opened the door wider so that Bel could come in.

"Please, then. Come in and be seated. I shall awake Ms. Harrison to greet you." The servant's words would've seemed more pleasant if only his tone of voice had been somewhat gentler. Bel found it awfully strange for her aunt to be sleeping at only five o'clock, but she shrugged it off and wandered into the sitting room.

When Aunt May wandered in, her shocked expression almost worried Bel. The silver haired woman stood in her blue wrapper before the sofa, on which they sat, and simply stared. Bel wished that she would hurry and say something so that they could get some much-needed slumber.

"So, you're my great niece, Belinda, eh? And I suppose that these are Toby and Dora. Hmm.. I never expected you so early but-"

"Please, Aunt May," Bel interrupted. "I don't mean to be rude whatsoever; but we've been walking through the cold, wind and snow since dawn, and we're terribly worn out. If you would be ever so kind to allow the children to go to bed, it would be highly appreciated; and I will stay up with you if you really need explanations," she pleaded, her green eyes wide and innocent. At first, Aunt May did not look impressed, but a gradual smile curved on her lips and she said:

"Girl, I already like your boldness. Of course the children can go to bed, but not until they have something to eat. They must be absolutely ravished from walking that whole way! I had no idea that you'd been traveling all day, and by foot! Well, let's go into the kitchen. Herman!" she cried. The snooty man entered the room, awaiting his orders. "Please take these children into the kitchen and make them something warm to eat and drink. Also, bring out Miss Harrison a warm cup of tea." Bel handed the groggy Toby to Herman, and told Dora to obey the man and do as she was told.

"Now," said Aunt May sitting next to Bel. "I invite you to take your gun and bag off. There's no need to have them now." Bel did as she was told and even took off her paletote, too. "Why have you arrived so early, young lady? I wasn't expecting you until March."

"Well, Mother fell terribly ill with scarlet fever, and . . ."

"Scarlet fever? My dear! Did the children catch it?!" cried Aunt May.

"Oh no, of course not. They weren't allowed even near Mother's bedroom the entire time she was ill." Aunt May then looked at Bel.

"What about yourself?" she asked concerned.

"No, I'm alright. I haven't come down with any symptoms and if I did catch it, I would be awfully sick by now . . . Back to my explanation; Papa went to look for the doctor and somehow never returned. Mother died early this morning forcing me to get the children away from the exposure and bring them here as fast as I could. This was the only way I knew how. So, we came here, hoping that you'd take us into your home, which is deliciously elegant in every way I could imagine. I have never seen such richness in my entire life," Bel breathed looking around at every carved figure and detail in the room around her. Aunt May frowned.

"I'm terribly sorry that you had to go through all of that, my dear. And at such a young age, too . . . Well, I'll try my best to make life easier for you around here. You know that now you no longer really have to look after the children, for we do have Herman."

"But I must. They don't know Herman, and most likely Toby will have a crying fit whenever Herman tries to touch him. It's a good thing that he was still half asleep when I handed him over, or there would've been a terrible racket," Bel explained. Aunt May shook her head sorrowfully.

"I don't see how you can be so calm and good-natured after you've been through so much, and so soon too," she said. Bel looked sadly upon her folded hands.

"I'm trying not to think about it anymore, Aunt May. It hurts too much . . ." The silence was broken by Aunt May clearing her throat and rising from the sofa.

"I'm sure you wish to get some sleep, so I will escort you to your bedroom. Herman can bring your tea up later. Follow me, Belinda." The two wandered up the winding stairwell and into a double-doored master bedroom. The floor was carpeted, the windows were draped with magnificent silks, and the king-sized bed in the center was a masterpiece! It was a canopy bed with beautiful white lace draping from the high oak posts. Was Bel really going to sleep in there? Thick, wonderful blankets covered the large bed to hide a soft goose-down mattress. These luxuries were ignored by Aunt May as she wandered to the old trunk at the food of the bed, but Bel stared around in complete awe.

Aunt May pulled a rather fancy looking nightgown and handed it to Bel. After many hesitations, Aunt May finally convinced the girl to wear to bed what seemed to be a ball gown to Bel.

Like a grandmother, Aunt May tucked Bel in the large canopy bed and kissed her forehead tenderly.

"I believe I'm going to like you a lot, Belinda. Have a good sleep. I won't wake you in the morning so that you may sleep in," she said, heading towards the double doors.

"Thank you, Aunt May, and may you have a wonderful sleep full of romantic dreams tonight," Bel said after her. The elderly woman turned around in the doorway.

"Romance? Ha!" and the strong willed, romance-hating woman

was out of the room, closing the doors behind her.

During breakfast, Aunt May decided to sit beside Bel to drink her tea so that she could continue their conversation from last night.

"You, Bel, are much more beautiful than I ever expected you to be, and that shall be wonderful news for Michael," Aunt May said, clasping her hands together. Bel raised an eyebrow.

"Michael?" she queried. Aunt May was shocked!

"Dear me, child! Do you not know the first name of your fiancé?!" she cried.

"No, nor his last."

"Oh, I was sure your father had told you . . . Oh well. His full name is Michael Benjamin Avery. His father owns a wonderful fur coat company over in jolly ol' England. Mister Avery is quite wealthy, too you know . . . I made sure to pick a decent man for you, and indeed I did. He is of extremely good manners with a proper upbringing, and he knows what to do in almost any difficult situation. He's a stubborn one, though, and he almost always gets his way if he sets his mind on something," she explained, stopping to take another sip of tea. "This Mister Avery sounds like a spoiled child to me, Aunt May," she boldly declared. Aunt May looked upon Bel with great interest.

"I may be an old spinster, but I know what I like, and I do like you. Although, may I suggest that you meet your fiancé before you label him, my dear?" Bel nodded. "Alright then. I'll let you finish up your meal and then I'm taking you and your siblings to the general store to pick out some new dress material. I'm sure you couldn't bring all of your clothing with you."

"Actually, we didn't have room for any," Bel said sadly. Aunt May almost laughed.

"That's alright, Belinda. I'll take care of it all," she said.

***

One cold, winter's morning a few days after their arrival, Bel wandered across the dusty snowy street towards the general store. A rather finely dressed young man appeared out of a building and accidentally bumped into the dazed girl.

"Oh, excuse me, Miss," he apologized, tipping his top hat. Bel recognized that the man had an accent; but not knowing how to determine accents, Bel had no idea where he came from. She assumed it was British from what her aunt had told her. "I didn't mean to knock you like that . . .Say, aren't you new around these parts?"

"Yes, Sir, I am," Bel replied, smiling politely. This young fellow was rather good-looking, tall, with blondish-brown hair, and noticeable blue eyes that Bel found to be dancing with excitement.

"Then allow me to introduce myself. I am Michael Avery." Bel's expression didn't change as it should have, but instead she continued to smile.

"Ah, so you're my fiancé!" Michael's square jaw dropped in disbelief, and when he finally closed his mouth again, he raised a nicely shaped eyebrow and said:

"That was rather brave of you to say, don't you think, Miss Harrison?" So the man did remember the name of his lovely bride to be! Bel didn't answer right away but just gazed at Mister Avery intently with that same lovely smile on her pink lips.

"To some it may be rather brave, but I was simply stating the truth Mister Avery, for you are, are you not, my fiancé?"

"Yes, you're right. Sorry to ever judge you, my dear," he teased, smiling. "I didn't expect you to be as stunningly attractive as you are. It surprises me," he said rather foolishly, "and not to mention your extreme boldness." Bel's cheeks reddened and she stood taller, and more firmly than before.

"Many people happen to admire my boldness," she snubbed.

"I'm not saying that it is a flaw, Miss Harrison . . .." There was an awkward silence, and Bel decided that it was about time that she was on her way.

"Mister Avery, I believe we should carry on this conversation some other time. I have to go to the general store to purchase some tea for Aunt May," Bel explained, beginning to wander in that direction. Michael almost seemed to panic for a moment, and shot his arm out to grasp hers, stopping Bel.

"Allow me to escort you there, Miss Harrison," he eagerly offered, still grasping her arm.

"Am I not too bold for you, Mister Avery?" she teased. Michael grinned. "Not at all, Miss. I happen to like it!" The two walked arm in arm into the store, and Bel bought the tea for Aunt May. She thanked Michael for his extreme politeness and quickly left his side to hurry back into the house, leaving an ecstatic, love-struck man in the middle of the snowy street.

***

One bright December morning, Bel was strolling down the street with her gloved hand slipped romantically through Michael's. It was a rather crisp morning, but Bel was prepared, dressed warmly for their outing.

Now that the children were settled in quite nicely, Bel decided that it was about time that she could leave them in the hands of Aunt May and Herman without worry.

The two wandered gaily past the general store, the bar, and the fur packing station, until they came to the front gate. Usually, Michael and Bel took walks around the forest outside of the Fort, but they had to wait for some men to enter before they could exit. Bel watched with extreme curiosity as two guards tried to drag in a ranting, raving, and screaming man! The man's clothing was torn something awful, his dark hair shaggy and his beard not trimmed. He seemed to be upset over something; and as he neared, Bel saw that the poor man was crying!

"What a lunatic," spat Michael. "I bet they're taking him to the jail house. He deserves to go there." Bel turned on Michael fiercely.

"How dare you say that?!" she cried. "You don't even know the man! He may be the kindest, nicest man you've ever met!" Michael took a step back, shocked.

"Bel? Why are you getting so upset?" she looked at the man one more time and this time, she saw him in a different light. He was familiar somehow, and as he came only a few feet away, the dirty man glanced up at Bel, and his face lit up. It was her father.

"Oh!" she cried, tears beginning to form.

"Bel! What's the matter!" Michael demanded.

"That's my father," she stammered. She attempted to reach out to Isaac, but the guards dragged him away. Isaac began to cry out Bel's name and Bel began to break down emotionally.

"Oh, Papa!" she yelled, running behind him. Michael caught up to Bel, but as they reached the jailhouse, the heavy wooden door was slammed in their faces. Bel stood outside the jailhouse with Michael, staring up at the barred windows in horror.

"They put him in there?" she asked. Michael nodded. "I'm glad you're here with me, Michael. I don't think I'd have the nerve to go in if you weren't beside me." He smiled. Finally, Bel was beginning to trust him and open up to him. After all their encounters, Michael finally felt like Bel's fiancé.

"I'm here," he soothed. "Are you sure you want to talk to him, Bel?" She nodded

"I must. I can't leave this unsolved," she whispered. Michael opened the door and the two entered the building and confronted the guard, to explain their situation. He believed them and led them to the cell where the sad, miserable man sat with his head in his hands.

"Papa?" she asked once the guard left them to be alone with Isaac. The man looked up, in disbelief it seemed, and stood, silent. "Papa, it's me, Bel." Isaac ran to the gate and put his arms through the bars, wanting to embrace his daughter.

"Bel!" he cried, his tears falling again. Without hesitation, Bel flung herself into his arms the best she could with the bars in the way. He held her for the first time in weeks.

"Oh, Papa," she said. "I've missed you terribly! Where have you been?" Isaac let go of Bel, and stood back, embarrassed to tell her what had happened.

"Bel, I'm ashamed to tell you."

"Please, Papa! I need to know, or I'll go mad!" she exclaimed. Saddened deeply by having to admit what happened, Isaac sat down on the bench in the cell and began to sob again.

"I did go mad," he almost whispered, his voice quivering. "When I returned with no doctor, I found your mother dead and went mad. Oh, Bel, you know how much I loved her, and I still love her. I couldn't handle the fact that the very breath within her had stopped . . . that she would never be coming back to hold me again. She would never speak to me again . . . I sat in the chair next to her bed, for how long I don't know, and then one day, two wandering hunters found me and dragged me away kicking and screaming. I just didn't want to leave her." Tears streamed down Bel's cheeks just thinking of her father going through all of that. "After that, I don't remember. Everything seems to be one big blank, and it almost pains me to try to remember. I knew you were here and that it would disgrace you to see your father like this, so I fought my best to stay away. The hunters overpowered me . . ."

"I'm going to get you out of here," she said, determined. Bel turned to Michael, desperately. "Will you help me?" she asked. Michael, willing to do anything for his love, nodded.

"I'd do anything for you," he whispered. Bel smiled.

"Thank you, Michael." Isaac rose from the bench and approached Michael, smiling. He put his arm through the bars, extending his arm.

"Hello, son-in-law," Isaac said. Michael grasped Isaac's hand and they shook firmly.

"Nice to meet you, Mister Harrison. I'd like you to know that you have one wonderful daughter." "I know," he replied, smiling with pride at Bel.

Bel explained the entire story of her journey and greeting with Aunt May. When she finished, Michael returned with the guard.

"Well," he said, "Mister Harrison, you're free. This young man here did a fine job of explaining things." The guard unlocked the gate and let out the weary, tired man who embraced his daughter the second that he was free from the iron bars. It was a happy moment, and once again, Michael was one step deeper into Bel's secret past.

The three strolled blithely into Aunt May's house, and boy was Aunt May surprised to see her nephew standing there, dressed horribly with such an unshaven face. In no time, Isaac was clean shaven, dressed in his uncle's old clothing, and smelling wonderful for the occasion. The occasion of a family reunion. What an incredible day!

***

The warm spring's sun joyfully warmed the pulled back shoulders of a jubilant bride, Belinda Harrison Avery. Even though she wasn't able to dress in a fancy, beautiful gown of white satin (it was a small wedding), her blue poplin was good enough for her.

The proud groom inside the government building signed the paper, while Isaac, Aunt May, Dora and Toby stood happily behind. The judge announced the marriage and Mister and Mrs. Avery were set to leave.

Away the happy couple rode, down the street in a buggy to Michael's large home. His house, however, was not a permanent one, for Michael planned to take Bel to his real home in London, England, the following week.

Bel was incredibly happy. No longer did she have to worry over her siblings or fret over the safety of their future. She now had her own future to look forward to. Bel's dark days were finally over and only bright, sunny skies lay ahead of her, shining as far as her green eyes could see.

A White Man's Duty

Sid Hughes

"They arrested that Indian of yours," Gibson said.

Jake Barnes said nothing, just stared at the miner for a moment, and then walked fast down Glisterton's dirt street, towards the town's jail. The 'jail' was actually a willie-house, a deep pit in the ground with a wooden floor and heavy logs across the top.

John Mitchell, an American, stood guard over the pit with a rifle. Barnes walked to the edge of the pit and looked through the gaps between the logs. Inside, in the darkness, he could sense a pair of near-black eyes staring silently into him. The prisoner said nothing.

"What did he do?" asked Jake.

Mitchell spat. "A bunch of redskins murdered a camp of railworkers, and last night we found C.J. Cashmore dead. Everyone says your Indian here killed him. We're waiting for Judge Begbie to put him on trial, and then we'll hang the Siwash bastard."

Glisterton was like any of the tiny goldmining camps that had sprung up along the gold-bearing creeks of the Cariboo. They would thrive until the gold dried up, leaving only a ghost town, the buildings rotting, eaten away by rain and frost until there was nothing left. Glisterton was mostly tents and shacks, with three saloons, a Blacksmith's, a General store, and a Whorehouse. It also had a thief.

C.J. Cashmore followed other men, watched them until they buried their gold, and then he'd steal it. Nobody had ever seen him put a pan in the water, but he kept coming to town with gold — right after someone would 'lose' his. Everyone knew C.J. was a thief, but nobody could prove it. Now Jake figured C.J. had stolen the wrong man's poke, and that wrong man had killed him for it.

Jake needed to think. He walked away from the willie-house

without a word. He passed silently up Glisterton's single street, towards his business, a pack-outfitting shop. He passed by his two rental mules numbly, entered the tent that was his shop, went around the ornate oak table in the centre, and dropped on his bed at the back of the tent. Someone had been murdered; Injun Joe was about to be tried by the roving "Hanging Judge" of BC — and Barnes knew Injun Joe was totally innocent.

Jake Barnes had met Injun Joe in Hope, after coming up the Fraser River on a side-paddle steamboat from New Westminster. Hope was as far as the steamers could go - beyond Hope, there was the Fraser Canyon. After the Royal Engineer-designed colonial order of New Westminster, Hope was a let-down. The town was barely more than a wharf on a river, a few rough, badly-painted wood buildings, and a sprawl of tents.

It was here that Barnes realized he had absolutely no idea how to get to any of the mining camps. He stood with his newly bought mules in the muddy street, a light drizzle wetting everything in sight. There was a crack of thunder, and the rain began to pour down in sheets, kicking up mud and creating puddles everywhere. Barnes ducked into a saloon, one of the few wooden buildings, for shelter and a few drinks.

The place was warm, relatively dry, and smelled of tobacco, alcohol, and cedar. The noise of conversation and laughter nearly covered the rain hammering on the shingles above. The walls were made of roughly-cut boards, thick with splinters, saw marks, and dried sap. The floor was a layer of fresh sawdust that soaked up spilled beer, tobacco juice, and the water that dripped through the roof.

As Jake sipped his drink at the bar, someone spoke behind him.

"You need a guide," the voice said. It was a statement, not a question. Jake turned around and looked at the speaker. He was an Indian, glazed-eyed and swaying from side to side. He had long, stringy hair down to his shoulders, and a scarred, weathered face.

"Are you any good?" Jake asked. The man beside Jake at the bar, a big lumberjack, coughed.

"That's Injun Joe," the man said. "He's a drunken Siwash most of the time, but a good guide when he's sober. Give him two bottles of whiskey and he'll get you through — but don't give him the bottles until he gets you through." The logger turned away and concentrated on his beer. Jake took a slow sip from his whiskey.

"Joe," he said, "you're hired. We leave tomorrow." Joe nodded, silent.

The next morning, as the previous night's storm faded away to another drizzle, Injun Joe appeared. He helped load Barnes' mules, and the two left Hope behind them and started their long journey up the Fraser Canyon.

The canyon was impossible to travel by boat. The river was narrow, treacherous, and fast, but the canyon led directly into gold country. The prospectors, being unable to ride the river, decided to walk along beside it. Logs were hammered into the sides of the canyon and planks laid down on top to form a sturdy but slick walkway, often more than a hundred feet above the river below.

Barnes and Injun Joe made their way along the walkway towards the Interior. Joe was silent, just as he been since Barnes met him, so Jake walked, the dull thudding of boots and hooves on the planks the only thing disturbing his thoughts.

Jake Barnes was what they called a 'remittance man' — a son of a wealthy English family sent away to the colonies for disgracing the family name. His taste for drink had been barely tolerated by his family, but his addiction to gambling had been the last straw. A run of bad cards had lost enough of his family's money to have him sent to New Westminster, a tiny colony on the west coast of British North America. Every month, or whenever the ship arrived, Barnes received a remittance from his father — enough money to keep him living comfortably, but far away from the family that he had shamed. His life continued thus until his father was ruined in a land speculation scam. Jake's stipend disappeared, so he sold everything he owned, bought two mules and enough wares to start a store, and set off on a steamer to the Cariboo.

The swollen Fraser River blasted through the canyon with the fury of a circus lion released into a crowd. The rains had made the boards slick, but Jake was reflecting with a grim chuckle on the events that had taken him from his wealthy life in Britain to his current pathetic situation. Then he slipped, and Jake slid off the walkway, too startled to even yell.

Somehow, his hand caught the edge of the walkway, twisting his arm and leaving him dangling far above the white water below. A shot of pain ran up and down his back. With an effort of sheer will, Jake brought his other hand onto the slimy planks and clawed for a grip.

Wind and spray from the boiling river whipped into his hair and eyes. His hands slipped on the slimy boards, and he nearly slid off into the thundering river. He looked down at the violent, roaring water below, and then back up at Injun Joe. Jake's two mules, with enough supplies to outfit several miners, stood idly next to the Indian. As Jake tried to dig his fingernails into the boards for some grip, he knew that Joe could leave him to die, take Jake's mules, and live comfortably. The roaring water below seemed to want to laugh, eager to swallow him, and beat him to death. His muscles ached. His grip began to weaken.

Injun Joe reached down. His right hand grasped Jake's, and pulled him onto the boards, only a slight grunt disturbing Joe's characteristic quiet. The two stared at each other for a moment. Fine droplets of rain blew past. A mule snorted. Both were silent.

"I owe you my life," Jake said. "I will forever be in your debt."

More silence.

"Let's keep moving," Jake decided. They resumed their walk above the river. They walked for nearly an hour before Injun Joe spoke.

"You're welcome."

Glisterton was the first camp they reached. The streams were rich in gold and new miners were appearing every day, so Barnes opened his store quickly. He rented out his two mules by the day, sold bags, tents, pots and pans, and everything else a prospector would need. He made Injun Joe a full partner - Jake sold pack, and Joe could guide prospectors around the hills, or back to Hope. The business made enough to allow the two to live well, by mining-town standards. Every so often, Barnes and Injun Joe would invest some of the store's profits in a few bottles, and the two would go into the woods and get drunk. Their weakness for alcohol was their bond, and eventually they became as close friends as drinking buddies can.

They had been drinking the night of the murder. There was no way Injun Joe killed Cashmore — it was just convenient for the miners to let an Indian drunkard be hanged in the real murderer's place.

Someone was entering Jake's store. Jake got to his feet and made his way to the front. It was Gibson. He sat on the scuffed, but still exquisite, wooden table in the center of the tent.

"So, the redskin murdered C.J. Can't say I'm not grateful for his choice of victims, but it's just like those ungrateful savages to knife the white man in the back, after all we've done to help them. " Gibson said cheerfully. "Where did you get this desk, anyway?"

"Gibson, Joe didn't do it," said Jake. Gibson chuckled.

"Sure, you say it, but how can you be sure? He's a Siwash, for God's sake. They have no respect for anything."

"He was with me all night. We were drinking. I bought the whiskey at Jim Beam's saloon, Jim would remember. Joe couldn't have killed C.J." Gibson's normally lively face hardened into a grim mask, and his voice was ice.

"Now listen to me, you fool," said Gibson. "That redskin is going to hang, understand? We don't know who killed C.J. He cheated us all sometime or another. Maybe that murder shouldn't have happened, but it did, and us white men have to stick together. Judge Begbie arrives tomorrow, and Joe will hang."

"Leave my store, sir," said Jake quietly. Gibson looked like he would say more, then shook his head, and went out into the evening air.

Jake left his store and walked across the street to Jim's, a large, dirty canvas tent. Inside, it was gloomy, but dry and warm. Jake ordered whiskey, and Jim silently poured a glassful and moved away. Several miners were clustered around the bar. As one, they raised their glasses and cheered.

"What's going on?" asked Jake. One of the men turned to face him.

"Well, we're lifting a glass to the memory of C.J. Cashmore," said the miner, pointing to a few men around him. He pointed to a few more men down the bar. "They're toasting that Indian for killing him. Then we switch," laughed the man, and turned away.

Jake threw back the whiskey, and then a few more, trying not to hear the laughter.

He decided to talk to Injun Joe.

When he left the bar, thick clouds were darkening the sky. At the willie-house, Mitchell stepped into his path, clutching his rifle.

"You can't see him," Mitchell growled. The sky rumbled distantly.

"Why not?" demanded Barnes, looking around.

"I talked with Gibson. You'd better make up your mind, Barnes. You have to decide whose side you're on. Are you with us, or them?"

"I owe my life to Injun Joe," Jake said.

"He saved one man's life and took another," grated Mitchell. "Doesn't matter, he'll still hang." Mitchell, in a long speech, told Barnes that white men, in a land full of savages, had to give their first loyalty to their own kind. "Those redskins are murdering people up and down the Kulmat-whatever that river is. You trust them, you end up dead, just like those workers."

Jake went back to his store. Night was falling fast. Slowly, numbly, he lowered himself onto a cot. For hours he tossed and turned. Eventually, he fell into a black sleep.

In his dream, Jake was tied to two massive horses, each pulling in the opposite direction. One was a deep red, and the other white. The pain was unbearable, but the two horses kept pulling, harder and harder, until Jake was sure he was going to be torn in two — and Jake awoke with a start. Rain rustled down the sides of his tent, and a clap of thunder shook the air.

"The Judge! The Judge is here!" someone yelled from outside.

Jake went out of his tent, and into the storm. Water glistened everywhere. The scudding sky unleashed its tons of rain onto the land. In the street, some miners were struggling in the mud, erecting the tent to serve as the courthouse. Others were hammering together a gallows. Gibson came up to Jake, rubbing water out of his eyes and hair.

"Barnes! We want that pretty table of yours for the judge's bench," he laughed. Already two miners were manhandling the table out. Gibson directed them away towards the court-tent. Jake followed, hunching against the wind.

The tent was set up, furnished, and the judge entered. Begbie was known for his fairness, except murder. Begbie hanged murderers immediately, no exceptions.

"All rise!" called Begbie's secretary, and the crowd in the tent lumbered to its feet. Begbie walked purposefully to Jake's table, and sat behind it, on one of the bar's stools. The crowd sank to their seats.

"This proceeding is begun," Begbie announced. "Bring forth the accused." There was a rustle from the rear of the tent, and Injun Joe, dirty, wet, and cold, was brought to stand in front of the bench. Judge Begbie looked at the indictment and cleared his throat.

"Ah, Injun Joe, you are charged with the murder, in cold blood, of Christopher Jacob Cashmore. If you are convicted you will hang, do you understand?"

Injun Joe was silent. Jake trembled slightly in his seat. Even though Joe was facing the judge, he felt as if the Indian were somehow watching him, expecting him to speak up. Jake looked around the crowd and saw many of the people were staring at him, watching to see what Barnes did. Begbie sighed.

"Injun Joe, how do you plead?"

Silence. Rain beat hard on the sides of the tent.

"Have you no words to speak in your defense? Has anyone any evidence to present?" Jake could feel the townspeople's eyes burning into the back of his head. Joe turned his head slightly, as if to look at Jake, but turned back to face the Judge. Now the eyes of the entire town were focused on Jake.

Jake clenched his teeth and kept silent. Joe turned.

Joe looked straight into Jake's eyes, his face an unreadable mask. Slowly, Joe lifted his hand, stretched it out to Jake, asking the man he had saved to save him. Jake looked away, torn, unable to decide. Joe turned back to face the judge.

"Guilty," Joe said. An icy hand stole into Jake's chest and crushed his heart. The crowd gasped in unison, then a silence fell over the court. Only the sound of the rain outside could be heard. Then Begbie cleared his throat.

"Very well then, this court sentences you to be hanged by the neck until you are dead, sentence to be carried out immediately." Two men took a hold of Joe and walked him outside. Begbie rose and left the tent. The people followed. Jake was left alone. He slumped. His stomach twisted.

There was scuffling from outside. Jake lay on his back silently, studying the rough canvas of the tent dully. He felt a scream clawing its way out of him, almost making it, before dying, sliding slowly back into his gut. It had all gone wrong. He rose shakily to his feet.

Rain fell lazily from the sky, swept sideways by the occasional gust of wind. The fresh timber of the gallows glistened. Joe, hands bound, stood on the gallows, the entire town gathered around. Jake moved through the crowd, came as close to Joe as he could. The noose was placed around Joe's neck, and a bag was pulled over his head. A clap of thunder and the faint hiss of the rain were the only sounds.

Jake knew Joe's eyes were staring into him through the bag, accusing him, seeing his cowardice. Jake felt sick. Out of the corner of his eye, he saw Begbie nod, some mechanism was worked, and the trap door beneath Joe's feet dropped away.

The Indian dropped a few feet and stopped with a jerk and a snap. He grunted and kicked his legs involuntarily as the rough rope took the life from him. Jake could not tear his eyes away. Droplets of water shook from Joe as he wrenched. One landed on Jake's lip.

A few more minutes and the body was still, hanging limply from the rope. A low cheer rose slowly out of the crowd. Jake stood, unable to take his eyes from the pathetic lump of dead flesh and rope.

Gibson and Mitchell came up beside him.

"You did the right thing, Barnes," said Gibson. "You did your duty." Jake nodded numbly. He felt strangely distant, far away from his own body.

"Let's get a drink," said Mitchell. They walked away from Joe's corpse. The saloon tent was slowly filling. Jake walked over to the bar and rested his head against the worn surface.

"Jim! Give this man a whiskey - a lot of them," called Gibson. Jim grunted and laid out a line of grimy shot glasses. The line ended at Jake's head. Jake heard the amber liquid gurgling into the glasses.

He raised his head. His hands reached up and took the nearest glass, as if it were someone else's hands. The hands put the glass to his lips. Distantly, he felt the whiskey burn its way down, then try to come back up. His head dropped back onto the bar, hard enough to cause the glasses to jump. He liked the jolt of pain from the impact - it was real.

Jake turned his head till he could see the line of drinks, stretching away into his future, when his heart would stop and he would join Joe somewhere dark.

His hand reached for the next glass.

Facing Change

Erika Manthey

Chapter 1: Water

The sun peered into Jeffrey's room, sending streaks of light onto the hardwood floor. Outside a lone rooster crowed from the top of a crooked fence post. The animals on the farm began to wake up and move about. The cows were bellowing to be milked, and the horses were nickering to be fed. Inside the modest farmhouse, a fire roared in the stove and bread was being made for the day. Jacob Bailer was eating his eggs and toast at the wooden table across the room from the stove.

Susan, Jacob's wife, was busy kneading the dough for the bread, and at the same time watching Josee, to make sure that her porridge went into her mouth instead of onto the floor.

"Do you think it's really a good day to cut the hay, Jacob?" questioned Susan, as strands of chestnut colored hair fell across her flushed face.

"I'm going to have to; this is the first clear day we've had in weeks and we can't wait any longer. The horses' feed is getting low and it's almost time to pay the farm hands again," he replied, while taking another slice of toast in his large, work callused hand.

It was already late August and the second cut of hay had not been taken in. The first cut had been a disappointment compared to last year's crops. It had been just too wet this year and there had not been enough sun.

Jacob pushed his plate away and drank back the rest of his orange juice. He got up from the table and walked over to where his young, three year old daughter was sitting, slurping back her porridge. In spite of Susan's efforts, Josee still managed to drop handfuls of porridge onto the floor.

Jacob smiled down at Josee with sad eyes, "Ah, my little darling, if only I could be as carefree as you." Josee gurgled and cooed in response, offering a small handful of porridge to her father.

"Don't worry Jacob," assured Susan, " this cut is bigger than the last and richer too. It should carry us through the winter at least."

"That's what I'm hoping for; if the weather cooperates, we'll be alright," he replied. He bent down to give Josee a kiss on the head and walked over to the coat rack to get his coat and hat. Despite the fact it was late summer, it was still fairly crisp early in the morning. As he was putting on his coat, his son came sauntering into the kitchen, rubbing his sleepy eyes.

"So Jeffrey, you finally decided to wake up and show yourself," Susan teased, getting a bowl from the cupboard for him.

"You better hurry up and eat your breakfast son, because we've got a lot to do today. Starting with milking the cows. That'll be your job today, along with mucking out the stalls and feeding the horses. The boys and I will be cutting the hay and I'll need you to help out."

"Ah, Pa! Me and Jimmy were going to go to the fishin' hole today and catch that monster fish in there! An' I'm feelin' lucky today too!"

"That fish will just have to wait Jeffrey because we're cutting hay today and you're helping, whether you like it or not," Jacob gave his son a look that brooked no argument and turned around and went out to the barn.

Jeffrey slumped down into one of the wooden chairs at the kitchen table, sighing. He maintained a scowl on his face while he ate his breakfast. He had really wanted to go fishing today. Jimmy's Pa never made Jimmy stay at home and work on nice days.

"Your Pa loves you very much Jeffrey, he doesn't mean to be rough with you." Susan walked over and put her arm around him, "It's just the times we're in are getting hard. Now you hurry up and get dressed; there's a lot to be done today." She gave her son an affectionate kiss on the head and shooed him off.

***

The sun was high in the sky and Jacob's coat and hat had long since been removed and put away. Beads of sweat adorned his forehead and stained his red shirt a darker shade on the front and back.

The hay was half done, and the men were getting ready to go in for lunch. Everyone was hot, sweaty and covered in dust from the hay.

The men were pulling their kerchiefs from the back pockets of their worn overalls and patting their faces and necks. Jacob's neighbor, Thomas Aison, had removed his sweaty shirt. He was sitting by the well in just his pants and undershirt, wiping his face with a kerchief he had soaked in water.

Jeffrey had just finished mucking out the stalls and brushing down the horses and now he was carrying a bucket to the well to get water for the horses; who were thirsty from pulling the hay cutter all that morning.

"Jeffrey, you're old enough to be helping with the hay now, and you're a good size too. How old are you now, boy?" Thomas asked stuffing his wet kerchief back into his pocket.

"I'll be thirteen come fall, sir. An' I'd like to help with the hay, but Pa told me to do the barn chores today 'cause he wanted the older boys to help in the fields."

Jeffrey lowered the bucket into the well to scoop up some of the fresh water; then, he removed it slowly, so as to avoid spilling the water out.

"Jacob, why not have the boy drive the horses after lunch?" Thomas suggested. His blue eyes sparkled against his weathered skin.

Jacob looked up at Thomas; then at Jeffrey, he pondered the idea for a few moments, then nodded and said, "Alright, we could use another hand." He pressed his kerchief against his forehead to soak up the beads of sweat that lingered there.

An excited smile broke across Jeffrey's face, and his heart began to beat a little faster. He had never driven the horses before, never while they were pulling the hay cutter. Pa always said that Jeff wasn't strong enough.

"Are you done all your chores, son?" Jeff's father asked, trying not to smile in amusement at his son's reaction.

"Yes, sir! " Jeffrey said trying not to sound too excited, not wanting the other men to laugh.

"Good, now it will go all the faster," Thomas said in a matter of fact way.

"Well boys let's go get some grub." Thomas slapped his knee, stood up and began to walk towards the house. There was a dark splotch on his pants where he had put his kerchief.

Jacob shoved his kerchief into his pocket and stood up. The other men got up from where they were lying on the grass in the shade, and some of them were laughing at a joke one of the men had made about Thomas' pants. Jeff, still smiling, emptied the bucket of water from the well into his own bucket. The water splashed and spun, like a raging river caught between two walls of rock. Some of the water splashed up onto Jeffrey's pants, leaving dark stains wherever it came into contact. The water felt good on Jeffrey's legs; it was a very hot day and Jeff was aching to go swimming down at the swimming hole. He looked out across the acres of rolling fields, with feelings of pride and responsibility surging in his chest. One day this would all be his. He was going to make this farm the best, most prosperous farm in the valley.

"What's the matter, boy, you tired from that little bit of work today?" Jacob joked, stepping out onto the veranda, "I thought it might be a bit much for you, but it did you good." Jacob sat down in a chair near the swinging seat that Jeff was lying on. He set his drink on the table between them and leaned back to look out at the starry night sky.

"I never knew how much work you had to put into a farm to get something back from it," Jeff stated in a far off voice, as if he were talking to the whole universe in general. "I always thought no matter what, the hay would be there, and the chickens would lay eggs, and the cows would give milk; but it's so much more than that. You've gotta work the soil, cut the hay and fertilize the fields. I mean, I always knew that, but I just never really thought about it until today. When I was out there in the fields with you guys and we were working together I felt as if everything should stay the same and never change." Jeffrey's voice trailed off as he pondered about the things he had just said. His deep brown eyes were looking out at the clear night sky, and a light breeze toyed with his fine brown hair.

Meanwhile, Jacob was lost in his own thoughts, his eyes looking out at the same stars as his son's. Sadness overcame him; his son had said so much without realizing the pain that it had inflicted upon his father, each word stinging like a burning hot tear.

Although the hay would cover them for the winter, there would be major changes. Jacob didn't want to admit it, but if anything happened to the hay, they were doomed. They would have to sell the farm for sure. He had talked it over with Susan, and they had decided that their horse, Joxer, would have to go in order to pay the farm payment in April. Joxer was Jeff's horse; he was a sturdy chestnut Clydesdale with huge feet and an amazingly long mane and tail. He had been Jeff's horse since the moment Jeff set eyes on him at an auction five years ago. Now he would have to go because he was the only thing that Jacob and Susan could think to spare, aside from the pigs. They had already decided to slaughter them in the spring for meat.

Only the darkness of the night hid the sadness in Jacob's eyes. Tonight he seemed a little older and a little more stooped in his chair, as if the weight of the world rested on his shoulders. Jacob didn't know how to tell his son that they would have to auction Joxer. He didn't have to tell him tonight anyway. Sooner or later Jeff would realize that his parents were worse off than they were letting on. It would probably happen sooner rather than later; Jeff was a smart boy and he would be able to figure it out before long. Then Jacob would have to tell him their plan to sell Joxer. But for now, all was peaceful, and Jacob pushed his thoughts of a bleak future to the back of his mind where, hopefully, they would stay. His eyes scanned the heavens; a sense of peace covered him like a sheet of silk; penetrating to his core and soothing that nagging feeling in the pit of his stomach.

Meanwhile, inside the house, Jeff could hear Josee's screams of delight as his mother splashed water on her little body during her bath. He could hear the crickets in the fields singing to the night. Jeff heard his father get up to go in for the night, then the creak of the screen door bumping as it shut behind him. Far to the west, he could see what looked like a thin strip of cloud in the enormous, starry sky.

***

Susan awoke to the soft pitter-patter of rain lightly tapping against the window. She lay quietly for a few moments, then her eyes flung wide open and she gasped loudly, "Jacob, the hay!"

Chapter 2: Earth (five years later)

From the hill, Thomas Aison could see a tall, slim figure step out of a weathered, black car. The boy looked to be about eighteen; he was wearing a tattered black suit with an old black hat and worn black shoes. Inside the car Thomas could see a young girl of about eight, struggling with an umbrella that was a touch too big for her. She had long, curly blonde hair, and her black dress looked a bit big on her. She had to lift it up above her ankles so that it wouldn't touch the ground as she got out of the car.

Even though their clothes were nothing to speak of, the pair looked relatively healthy. This was more than Thomas could say for the lady getting out of the car now, with the aid of the boy. She had thin, gray-brown hair, more gray than brown really, that fell in wisps about her face despite her efforts to pin it back. Her figure was lean, too lean, and her posture was stooped. Her face showed the stress of too many years. The bags under her eyes revealed that she had not slept properly in months.

Thomas' heart nearly broke; could this be the same family that had been his neighbors for so many years? Slowly he walked down the hill towards them, his eyes studying each of them in turn.

"Jeffrey?" Thomas asked hesitantly as he neared the tall, young man.

The boy turned around; his sad brown eyes lighting up a bit as he recognized his old neighbor. Thomas had lost a little weight since he had last seen him, and he seemed to have shrunk a bit too, but other than that he was the same old Thomas. "Hello Thomas, I'm glad you could make it. It wouldn't be the same without you here."

"We all made it Jeff, except my wife; poor Edith's in bed with a terrible flu," Thomas replied, looking from Jeffrey to Josee, "could this be little Josee? My word, you've grown girl, and a fine little lady you've turned out to be!"

"Thank-you sir," Josee said timidly, still having trouble holding her umbrella and keeping her skirt from touching the wet ground.

"Thomas, I'm so happy you could make it," a quiet voice said from behind Jeffrey. Susan stepped out and offered Thomas her thin hand.

"My condolences to you Susan. Jacob was a fine man; the best I've ever met. He'll be sorely missed." Sadness laced Thomas' voice.

"Thank-you Thomas; you don't know how much that means to me. I don't know what I'm going to do, now that he's gone." Her eyes began to mist; she was the saddest looking thing that Thomas had ever seen.

Her once clear, rosy skin now looked dull and lined. Her hair, which she had always kept so nice, was now gray, thin and lifeless. Her dress hung from her bony frame like a sheet draped over an old piece of furniture. All in all Susan looked as if someone had shut her up in a closet and forgotten about her.

"Everyone is waiting to give their condolences to you and the children, Susan. The pastor is here too; are you ready?" Thomas asked her carefully, not wanting her to break down right here.

The four of them walked solemnly up the hill to say goodbye to their husband, father and friend.

The weather seemed to suit the mood, dreary and depressed. Susan, Jeffrey and Josee stood in silence as the pastor spoke about the good man Jacob was.

When the pastor had finished his speech, Jeffrey stepped forward and raised his hand. The quiet whispering and bustling stopped;

only a few muffled sobs and sniffles could be heard. Everyone looked at Jeffrey; even the children were quiet.

"If you don't mind, I would like to say a few words about my father," a heartbreaking sadness hung in his voice. "My father was a good man. He was the fairest, most hard working man I've ever known. When our farm was taken from us five years ago, he never gave up the hope of someday buying it back. He was devastated when he had to send Josee and me to relatives because he couldn't afford to keep us. My father was determined to make enough money to start over again. The only reason why he went down the mineshaft that day was to get one more load, for five more cents. Five more cents that he could put away towards getting back our farm."

A sob escaped Susan's throat and tears streamed down her face.

"Due to my father's determination and hard work, we hardly ever felt the pang of hunger, although I'm sure that he felt it more often than we will ever know; because that's the kind of man my father was. He gave everything for us, including his life." Jeffrey paused for a moment and looked around at the red-eyed women leaning against their husbands and clutching their handkerchiefs in their hands. The men bore grim faces; some of them had tears in their eyes. All of them held their hats to their hearts in respect for the good man who died under tons of hard unforgiving rock while hauling just one more load.

" I will never forget my father, and I can only hope that I will become half the man he was."

Jeffrey bent down and scooped up a handful of the fresh, black earth that lay beside his father's grave. With one reluctant movement, he opened his hand and dropped it onto his father's coffin, "I'll miss you Pa," Jeffrey whispered hoarsely, a single tear running down his cheek, "Don't worry about Ma and Josee; I'll take care of them now. Bless you Pa," Jeffrey turned around and walked away, away from his father, away from the tearful mourners, and away from his childhood.

Chapter 3: Fire

Susan knelt down in front of the altar in the great, old church. Candles burned softly at either side of her, casting holy light upon the Virgin Mary's angelic face. Baby Jesus lay in Mary's arms adorned with rich purple cloth. In the background, hymns could be heard, echoing through the great halls of the church. There were only a few other people in the church. They were sitting in pews, and praying for Jesus and Mary to carry them through this hard time. Susan wasn't any different; she had come this early winter morning to ask the Almighty for some help.

Tears ran down Susan's lined, tired face. The stress of Josee being sick was taking its toll on her. She bent her head and whispered her thanks. Susan stood up and before leaving, lit a candle for Jacob; as was her custom. Then she quietly made her way out of the church and onto the bustling street.

There were paperboys shouting out the morning news, and people opening up little shops. It was snowing lightly so Susan pulled her shawl tighter around her shoulders and started out on a brisk walk for the factory.

The whistle blew loudly, telling the women on the floor that the day was over and that they could go home. Susan shut down her machine and watched the little girls run around the floor picking up the fluffs of wool that had been scattered during the day. They shoved them into bags that hung around their necks; as other girls went from machine to machine switching the empty spools of wool with full ones. Josee used to be one of these girls, until she got sick and couldn't do it anymore. Susan noticed that a few of them coughed as they ran up and down the aisles collecting the precious wool. That's how it had started with Josee too.

Walking home, Susan began to think about their past life on the farm and how the fields looked in the morning when the sun was rising and the dew sparkled. She remembered the smell of fresh baked bread that always used to linger in the house until she opened the windows and let in the fresh, country air. She remembered Jacob.

Her eyes swelled with tears, she tried to blink them back but they came spilling out anyway. Quickly she searched her pocket for a handkerchief but found none, instead she brushed them away with the back of her hand, but it was no use. She thought that by this time she should have no tears left but they always seemed to come.

She felt the presence of someone walking up beside her.

"Beg your pardon miss, but could I offer you this?" A tall, slim man held a white handkerchief out towards her. His eyes were the clearest blue she had ever seen. He wasn't particularly handsome but he was by no means ugly. He had dark brown hair that was neatly combed to the side; he looked to be in his late thirties. His skinny frame was well dressed, and he wore a smile that was both kind and mysterious all at once.

"Thank-you, sir," Susan accepted, taking the handkerchief from the tall stranger. She dabbed her eyes and looked up at the man.

"My goodness! Pardon me, my name is Anthony Black, and who might you be?"

"I'm Susan Bailer. Thank-you sir, but I should be on my way. My daughter is sick and I must take her medicine to her."

"Sick you say? Has she seen a doctor?" Anthony Black questioned a look of concern flashing in his blue eyes.

"Yes, but not recently, I can't afford it you see," Susan looked down, blushing with embarrassment, "Now I really must be going; it's late and my son will be worrying before long."

"Please, allow me to walk you home, and if I may take a look at your daughter? I might be of some help. I studied to be a doctor for a year, before deciding to become a bookkeeper."

"Thank-you Mr. Black, but I couldn't trouble you; I'm sure you've got things to do."

"No trouble at all Mrs. Bailer. I'm happy to help," he replied, a smile lighting up his face. Susan and Mr. Black walked along the lamp-lit street, snow falling softly; covering their footprints and giving the world a hazy comfort.

"Jeffrey! The man went out of his way to help us! How can you not see that?" frustration edged Susan's voice.

"I don't like him Ma, showing up and being all nice; the man obviously has money. You saw the way he was dressed! What could he possibly want with us?" Jeff paced back and forth, a disgusted look on his face. He was trying to get through to Ma but she wasn't seeing it from his angle. She thought that the man was good and caring and very thoughtful. Jeff hated the fact that Mr. Black had never stopped smiling at her the whole time he was here. The truth was that Jeffrey was scared, scared that his mother might be forgetting Pa. Jeffrey slumped down into an old tattered armchair near the front window.

Josee came cautiously down the stairs clinging to the railing. Her frail body moved awkwardly as if she were just learning to walk.

"Josee! What are you doing? You could fall girl! Stay right there and I'll help you down the rest of the way," Susan ordered, amazed to see her little girl out of bed and walking down the stairs no less!

"Oh, Ma! I feel so much better this morning, can I go outside today?" asked Josee, eagerly. Her pale little face lighting with hope.

"Certainly not, young lady! You may be feeling better, but you're still not well enough to be running around outside yet." Susan couldn't help but laugh a little at the good spirits her daughter was in. Mr. Black's visit last night had really seemed to help Josee.

"Mr. Black was so kind, Ma. Is he going to come over again?" asked Josee as her mother helped her down the stairs. Jeff was sitting; scowling from the old armchair that he had slumped into.

"Possibly Josee; he was very nice, wasn't he?" Susan gave a quick glance at her son who was looking elsewhere; pretending not to hear what they were saying.

***

Outside it was cold and snowing heavily; it was December 19, 1936, and Christmas was just around the corner. There were holly and bows everywhere, and children were playing in the snow. Even though money was scarce for most, everyone was in the Christmas spirit.

Inside the small house, a wood fire was blazing, and the Christmas tree was being decorated.

"Susan, could you pass me that string of beads?" Mr. Black asked from where he stood surrounded by decorations waiting for their place on the tree.

Susan bent down and picked up the string of shiny red beads and handed them to Anthony. She had been so surprised when he knocked on the door this morning; holding a big box of decorations and a tree in the snow behind him.

Anthony had been coming over to check on Josee regularly. He and Susan had become closer all the while. When she invited him to have Christmas at their house, he was thrilled and said that he would bring something special for the kids. At the time Susan had no idea what he intended to bring, but she was overjoyed when she saw that it was a Christmas tree. Susan had no idea how she was going to afford to decorate one this year and make a good Christmas meal as well. She had been saving since October for this, and she now had enough to buy Josee the doll she had been talking about for weeks.

Jeffrey was nineteen this Christmas, and Susan intended to give him Jacob's old watch that he had left for Jeff. Jacob's own father had given him that watch and it was incredibly special to Jacob; he had wanted to see it passed on to his own son someday.

Josee helped Mr. Black set the string of beads on the tree; then she picked up a handful of the tiny clear glass icicles, "Oh, Mr. Black, these must have been very expensive! I'll be extra careful with them," her eyes were wide in wonderment. She had never seen glass icicles before and she treated them if they were newborn babies.

"They were my mother's, Josee; she got them when I was a little older than you. I imagine they were fairly expensive," Anthony replied, smiling. He looked up at Susan and winked, his blue eyes sparkling.

Susan watched Josee help Anthony hang the little icicles on the tree; she felt so happy. The house was so alive and festive again after the many dark, gloomy days. She noticed how well Josee looked. The shine and bounce had returned to her fair curls and the pink had returned to her cheeks. Susan, too, looked better. The shine had returned to her hair and the sparkle to her eyes. It was as if she were glowing from the inside out. Jeffrey no longer scowled every time the name Anthony Black was mentioned but just became a little more somber. Susan knew that he sorely missed his father, but he needed to move on.

"There, all done" Josee said, stepping back to admire the beautiful tree they had worked so hard on.

"No, not yet" Anthony replied, turning around and digging through the box. He pulled out a beautiful little angel. She had a sparkling golden halo above her head. It had to be the most beautiful little angel that both Susan and Josee had ever seen, for they both gasped.

"Come here Josee; I'll lift you up and you can put it on the top of the tree."

Josee walked over to Mr. Black, a look of wonderment on her face. He handed her the angel and lifted her up. She put it carefully on the very top of the tree and he set her back down. They all stepped back from the tree and looked at it; even Jeffrey came from the kitchen and stared along with them. It was fabulous! The light from the crackling fire made the ornaments sparkle and glow. Susan just stared at the beautiful little angel that sat on the tree looking down at all of them. The buzzer for the cookies that Susan had put in the oven earlier that morning went off.

"Oh, yum! The cookies are ready!" Josee squealed and ran off to the kitchen. Jeffrey followed her, not wanting Josee to try and take them out herself.

Susan looked up at Anthony and smiled," Thank-you Anthony, it's beautiful."

"There's no need to thank me. Come, let us join the kids in the kitchen," he replied.

When Anthony got up to get a game from his bag in the living room after their hot chocolate and cookies, Jeff got up to put the dishes on the counter. As he was setting the dishes down, he saw out of the corner of his eye Anthony bending over the small table in the living room. From where Susan and Josee sat laughing at the kitchen table they couldn't see what Anthony was doing, but from where Jeffrey stood at the sink he could. Anthony had picked up Ma's old, tarnished, gold watch that Grandmother had given her for her wedding present when she and Pa got married. He slipped it into his breast pocket and walked over to his bag to get the game he had promised.

***

Susan was just finishing brushing Josee's silky hair when she heard a knock at the door, "Jeffrey could you get it please?" She called out, but there was no answer, so she got up and smoothed out her dress, "How do I look Josee?" she asked, like a girl going out on her first date. Susan's hair was shiny and smooth; she had rouged her lips and darkened her lashes a bit.

"You're positively glowing Ma," Josee replied, smiling. She too had been allowed to put the tiniest amount of color on her lips, but nothing else.

Susan blushed and hurried to open the door. Standing before her in a crisp black suit was Anthony, holding three beautifully wrapped presents in his arms, "Merry Christmas!" he smiled; his cheeks and nose red from the cold.

"Merry Christmas to you too!" Susan returned, laughing. "Really Anthony, you didn't have to bring gifts."

"Nonsense! It's Christmas! Of course I'm going to bring presents!" He stomped his boots outside to remove the snow, then stepped inside.

Josee came from the kitchen her eyes widening at the sight of the neatly wrapped gifts. "My goodness Josee! You must be the prettiest little girl in the whole neighborhood! Here you go, Love, could you put these under the tree?" asked Anthony handing her the presents and grinning at her reaction.

Josee obediently took them over to the tree and began to arrange them with the other three her mother had put there that morning.

"Something smells good," Anthony remarked smiling at Susan.

"It's the turkey; I put it in this morning. It's not very big but it should be alright I hope." Susan was blushing now; why was Anthony looking at her like that? She smiled and asked; "Do you know what time it is? I seemed to have misplaced my watch. I think the turkey is almost ready."

"Of course; it's six o clock precisely," he replied, a mischievous smile crossing his face.

"Come and make yourself warm by the fire. I'll get you a cup of hot chocolate." she offered, turning and walking towards the kitchen.

"That's alright, I can get it myself; you're already making dinner." He followed her into the kitchen. The table was set with four places; in the middle two candles stood. A white tablecloth covered the old table and faded red napkins were lying neatly beside each plate.

Susan opened the oven and took out the turkey; it smelt delicious. On the stove, vegetables were being cooked, and a fresh loaf of bread lay cooling on the counter.

"Everything looks so good; you've outdone yourself, really!" Anthony exclaimed, looking at the food Susan had been preparing all day.

"I wanted this to be a perfect Christmas for the children; this is the first year we've really had anything to celebrate," Susan explained to him over her shoulder while putting the potatoes onto a plate.

"Really? What's that? Anthony questioned, curious.

Susan stopped, turned around and exclaimed, "Well, you of course!"

After dinner they all moved into the living room to sit by the tree. Jeff held Anthony back and warned, " Look, I know what you're up to so don't you go hurting Ma, or you'll have me to deal with."

Anthony's eyes widened in astonishment and he replied, "I would never hurt your mother Jeff; I'm only trying to help."

Anthony and Jeff joined Susan and Josee in the living room by the tree. Anthony seemed a little unsettled, and Jeff had a contemptuous look on his face.

"What do you say we open presents now?" Anthony suggested, forcing himself to smile and return some of the cheer that had been lost during Jeff's confrontation. He set down his hot chocolate and looked at Susan.

"Yah! Please Ma, please!" joined Josee, practically jumping out of her chair.

"I guess we could," Susan replied, smiling.

Anthony got up and picked selected two of the largest presents and handed them to Jeffrey and Josee. "It took me awhile to decide what to get for you; I hope you like it." The comment was directed more at Jeff than at Josee.

"Thanks," Jeff said, trying to sound happy, but he couldn't get the image out of his head of Mr. Black taking his mother's watch. He had probably used the money he had got from the watch to buy the presents.

Josee had practically ripped the paper off her present, but she forced herself to be careful because she wanted to keep the lovely wrapping paper. She pulled out a beautiful, blue dress; it had long sleeves and lace at the collar and it was made of the softest baby blue material.

She looked up at Anthony with shining blue eyes and said, breathlessly, "It's beautiful!" She held it up against herself and spun around, "Thank-you so much!" She ran over to where Anthony was sitting and flung her arms around his neck.

"Hoh-oh, you're very welcome Josee, but I won't take all the credit. Your mother helped me pick it out," Anthony laughed.

"Jeffrey, what did you get?" Susan asked, trying to see what Jeff held in his hand.

Jeff lifted it up; it was a beautifully bound book with a big, bold title written in gold lettering. Inside it contained full color pictures; each covered with a sheet of tissue paper to protect them.

"It was mine when I was about you age. My father gave it to me for my birthday. I wanted you to have it." Anthony said watching Jeffrey's expression.

"Thank-you, I'll keep good care of it," Jeffrey answered, looking in awe and the gift Anthony had given him. If Anthony hadn't used the money from Ma's watch to buy the gifts, then what could he have used it for?

"And for you Susan." Anthony lifted up the smallest of the presents he had brought with him and handed it to Susan.

She looked at him curiously, "What is it?"

"Open it and find out for yourself," he replied, a coy smile on his face.

Carefully Susan unwrapped the small gift. She removed the lid from the box and there inside was her watch, shining and gloriously new, " Anthony, you took my watch!" she laughed, pulling it out of the box, the sparkling gold catching the light of the fire.

"I saw how tarnished it was, and I thought you might like to see it looking new again," he said, smiling, pleased with how happy it made her.

Jeffrey stared at the watch then looked from his overjoyed mother to the smiling Anthony. He began to smile himself; the block of ice that he had formed against Anthony melted.

Susan gave Anthony a big hug and put her watch on her small wrist, her eyes shining, "I always meant to get it fixed up; I just never had the money for it, thank-you."

Josee gave a big yawn and everyone laughed. Looking at her watch, Susan exclaimed, "Oh my! It's far past Josee's bedtime! Jeffrey, would you mind?"

Jeffrey smiled and nodded, then picked up the half sleeping Josee and carried her off to bed.

Susan looked at Anthony, the blaze from the fire reflecting in his blue eyes.

"Susan," Anthony said quietly, looking at her carefully, "I've enjoyed every minute that I've spent with you, and I've gotten to the stage where, when I'm not with you, I can think of nothing but you." He looked deep into her eyes, and asked, "Susan, would you do me the honor of being my wife?" Hope shone from his eyes, and everything was momentarily silenced.

"Anthony, I feel the same towards you, but I would have to ask the children for their consent." She was looking equally as deep into his eyes.

Chapter 4: Air

The sun was shining down and the birds were singing sweetly. The smell of fresh country air and good food surrounded the murmuring guests. The music began; everyone simultaneously stopped talking and turned around. First Josee came; tossing flower petals into the air, her hair streaming down her back in abundant curls. Her beautiful baby blue dress made her look like a little princess. Following her was Jeffrey, dressed in a smart black suit, his hair combed neatly to the side. On his arm was his mother; wearing a simple white dress. Anthony had insisted on her getting something more extravagant, but she had flat out refused, "a simple white dress of a fashionable cut will do just fine. There's no need to spend extra money on something I'm only going to wear once," were her exact words.

Susan looked beautiful with her shiny hair pulled back in a twist. Her cheeks were pink with excitement, and her eyes shone with love as she walked down the isle.

While the priest gave his blessings Jeffrey looked from his mother to Anthony. They were so happy; he smiled for them.

A light wind rustled the leaves in the trees and played with Jeffrey's hair. The wind reminded him of that night so long ago when he and his father were looking out at the stars, and he knew in his heart that this is what Pa would have wanted.

WELCOME TO CANADA
CANADA

Caitlin's Promise

Chelsea Eby

They were leaving, the first time that anyone from the O'Connor clan had ever ventured from Ireland. She felt as if this ship, the Noreen, had ripped her from her mother's womb, leaving her a scared, helpless child to fend for herself in a new land. Gingerly, she placed her hand on her swelling stomach. This unborn child was her last tie to her homeland.

The cold, harsh wind slapped her in the face, bringing with it a wave of rain and sending the loose strands of her flaming red hair whipping wildly around her head. She pulled her wrap closer and stared at the rolling green hills of Ireland that were slowly shrinking into the distance. She had grown up in those fertile, protective folds, only to leave them.

As the markers of her lifetime faded away, she became lost in a sea of memories. She was jarred back to reality when someone squeezed her hand. She turned; her mind still somewhat lost, and looked confusedly at the small pale hand clasped in her own. She stared at the hand blankly, until her mind cleared, and realized it belonged to her son, Liam. She looked at him, and it was as if this was the first time she had seen him. He really was not a strong lad, she noted. He had been sick during infancy and had never really recovered. He reminded her of a newborn fawn; his pale, almost translucent skin was speckled with brown freckles, like a fawn's spotted coat. His big brown eyes looking out at the world with wonder and incomprehension, his face surrounded by a mop of soft, curly brown hair, and his small delicate body, smaller than most four-year olds, made her want to protect him from all the evils of the world. She gave his left hand a reassuring squeeze. He looked up at her and smiled, his small white teeth gleaming from between his pink lips.

Thinking this was a game; Liam squeezed his father's large hand and giggled. She smiled as her husband, Shamus, turned to her and said, "Caitlin, my dear, I swear that a monster just attacked my hand!"

At this, Liam burst into laughter and through his giggles, managed to say, "No Da, it wasn't a monster, it was me!"

Shamus laughed and turning back to look out over the waters, said, "You could have fooled me!"

It had been Shamus's idea to move to Canada. This burly man, who had passed to his son those kind brown eyes and soft brown hair, wanted to protect his family from the tensions of everyday life in Dungannon, another battle zone of Northern Ireland's religious warfare. He had also heard good things about employment in Canada. She had never been too keen on the idea, but here she was. Looking at his face she could see that his eyes sparked with excitement and anticipation. Off in the distance, over his shoulder, Caitlin could see the sun breaking through the clouds.

She turned back for one last look at the hills, but they were gone. Her steely gray eyes grew misty and she bowed her head, her salty tears mingling with the falling rain. After a little while Shamus said, "All right, let's get out of this rain." He picked up Liam and gently putting his hand on her shoulder whispered, "Come now love, it'll be all right."

He led her down the steps into the third class compartments. This had been all they could afford. They walked to their room, #147. Shamus opened the door onto a small room with a three-quarter bed, a desk, a lamp, a Catholic Bible, some bedclothes and their boxes of clothes that Shamus and the ship's crew had brought in when they had come aboard. Caitlin stood in the middle of the room and looked at the bleak quarters, the peeling, rusted walls, and painted metal floor. "We left our clean, beautiful home for this?" was all that she could think.

Shamus could see that his wife was upset, so he quickly said with a chuckle, "Not much to see here is there? Might as well see what else this ship holds, and meet the other passengers too!"

She tried to smile, but only nodded, not trusting herself to speak.

The other passengers of the ship were also out exploring. At the end of the hall, there was a dingy bathroom meant to service all the travelers. Upstairs, the mess hall consisted of two long tables set about with chairs, where all the third class passengers would be fed three meals a day. Next to the mess hall was the communal room furnished with a couple of couches, and some tables and chairs. This room was most likely where all the passengers would spend their time on this three-day journey. Already there was a group of people crowded around the short wave radio; the voice of U.S. President Kennedy filled the room. "How's that for the land of opportunity," a young, red-haired man asked, "where even an Irish Catholic can rise to power?"

"Here! Here!" came another voice from across the room.

Supper was not for another hour so the O'Connor family went back to their room. Inside, Caitlin looked at the bleak walls and said to her son, "Liam, would you like to make me some beautiful drawings to put up?"

Liam, who loved to draw, energetically responded, "Oh yes, Mum!" She took some crayons and paper out of one of the boxes and handed them to Liam, who excitedly went to work.

The hour passed quickly, but quietly; then the dinner bell sliced through the silence like a knife. They made their way through the crowded corridors to the mess hall, and found three seats together at the first table. Leaving his family to settle, Shamus got up to get his family their food from the buffet style meal line.

Sitting beside Caitlin was a large, three-generation family. The mother watched over her family of six children and their grandfather. The mother looked over and with a bright smile introduced herself, "Hello! I'm Muirin McLaugh, and this is my family."

As Shamus came with the food to sit down, Caitlin said, "A pleasure to meet you all. I'm Caitlin O'Connor, this is my husband Shamus, and our son Liam."

As the conversation progressed, the two families discovered that they were going to be neighbours for the next few days. Muirin's two youngest boys, Rory and Aidan, were around Liam's age. Liam, who was usually a shy child, quickly made friends with these two rambunctious boys.

Caitlin noticed throughout the meal that the grandfather didn't appear to be well. His breathing was raspy and he kept coughing, covering his mouth with a napkin. She looked at Muirin and asked, "What is wrong with your grandfather?"

Muirin lowered her voice as she answered, "The doctor back home said it was just a respiratory thing old people get, but I'm not so sure. That's one of the reasons why we're coming to Canada." During this conversation the grandfather had a fit of coughing. As he took his napkin away, Caitlin noticed in horror that there was blood on it.

The three-day trip stretched out to a week as the Noreen battled stormy seas. The two families became good friends in that short period of time, especially Liam, Rory, and Aidan. Caitlin realized that Muirin and her grandfather were just as excited as her husband about moving to Canada. He and Muirin spent most of the time talking about all the great things that Canada had in store for them, while Caitlin sat off to the side, wondering if she was the only one on this boat who dreaded her new life in Canada.

Although the McLaugh grandfather's condition worsened, and Liam caught a chest cold, there were still a great many things to laugh about, including Rory, Aidan and Liam's stories about what could happen in their new homeland. One night as Liam went to bed he told his mother about all the cowboys and Indians that were always fighting in Canada.

On the fifth day an unexpected event occurred; the McLaugh's grandfather died. A burial at sea took place and many passengers came out to pay their respects. Caitlin held Liam in her arms as Grandfather McLaugh's body disappeared under the waves. Liam, straddling his mother's pregnant girth, whispered into her ear, "Mum, do you have to die if you want to go to Canada?"

"No, of course not deary. Grandfather McLaugh was very sick, that is why he died," she replied, with tear filled eyes and a touch of sorrow in her voice.

When the Noreen reached its port in Montréal, Québec, and they cleared customs and immigration, the two families said their final farewells and tearfully parted. The McLaughs left for Toronto, to be reunited with Muirin's husband. The O'Connors were to stay in Montréal for awhile, with Father O'Malley, the brother of their parish priest. Father O'Malley met them at the port and helped them transport their luggage to his car. The noise and bustle at the port overwhelmed Caitlin; she found comfort in Father O'Malley's face amidst those of strangers, which was almost identical to his brother's.

After all their luggage had been packed into and onto his car, the O'Connors and Father O'Malley managed to squeeze in as well. Once inside, Father O'Malley spoke, "Well my children, how was your trip?"

His accent was barely discernable, which Liam duly noted, "Father O'Malley, your voice sounds funny."

The Father laughed merrily and said, "I'd have said the same thing to you!"

At this comment, Caitlin realized just how different they sounded to these Canadians. The thought of not hearing the soft lilt of the Irish language made her heart sink. With difficulty she replied, getting back to his question, "We lost a newfound friend; Liam contracted a chest cold, as you can tell by his coughing; and the storm that delayed us was rough..."

"But I didn't get sea sick like my friends" Liam piped up, causing everyone to laugh.

The chatter in the car stopped as Father O'Malley exclaimed, "Here we are!"

They were quickly set up in Father O'Malley's small, but cozy house. Their belongings were neatly piled away. Then, because they were exhausted, Caitlin and Liam went to bed. She sank thankfully onto the pillow and within minutes was asleep. While she and Liam slept, Shamus and Father O'Malley talked about their future life in Canada.

The next morning they accompanied Father O'Malley to his church for morning mass. Caitlin could sense the difference between her family and the other families here. Their clothes were different, and they talked differently. She looked about her nervously whenever Liam coughed, but despite her paranoia, no one seemed to mind.

When mass was over and still nothing had happened, she began to relax. Liam's cough had worsened since he had contracted it on the ship, so, feeling adventuresome, she decided to go out and get him some cough syrup. She asked Father O'Malley where there was a nearby chemist. He gave her the directions and smiled to himself as she walked away.

She reached the drugstore, opened the door and walked in, the door making a charming jingle as it closed. She looked about and finally found the aisle where the cough medicines were kept. Looking over the labels, she was distressed to find that she recognized none of these medicines. A woman, who was shopping nearby, noticed that Caitlin seemed to be having trouble finding a product, and came over to help.

"What are you looking for?" the woman asked.

"I'm looking for a medicine to relieve my son's cough." Caitlin replied.

As soon as the words left her lips the woman's face became hard, and thrusting the medicine into her hand hissed, "Go back where you came from, you bloody Mick! And take your disease infested kids back with you!" Caitlin was shocked. She stared with horror as the woman calmly turned on her heels and marched away. She paid for her purchase in silence and made her way home as quickly as possible.

Father O'Malley met her at the door. "Did you get what you wanted?" he asked kindly. At this question, all the emotions that had been building up inside her exploded in an angry, frustrated torrent of tears.

Father O'Malley, not expecting this reaction to his question, wrapped his arms around her and said, "There, there, my child, what's wrong?"

The whole story came tumbling out, how she didn't really want to be here, how she was afraid of being treated, how she had been treated today, even though she had begun to think things weren't going to be as bad as she had thought. Once these thoughts and emotions that she had been bottling up for so long were off her chest, she began to calm down. As her sobs quelled, she looked up at the Father. His blue eyes were kind and sympathetic. "I'm sorry Father, I don't mean to trouble you..." she began, but he interrupted her.

"Don't excuse yourself Caitlin, you're allowed to feel this way. Don't worry. Not everyone is so hostile. You unfortunately met one of the few people who are. But don't judge everyone you meet here based on your unfortunate meeting."

"Yes Father," she replied, managing a smile.

That night, as they were getting into bed, Shamus announced that Father O'Malley had spoken to a friend of his in Kamloops, British Columbia, who had set up a place for them to live and a job. "We'll be leaving tomorrow Caitlin, on the four o'clock train. Aren't you excited?" he exclaimed.

Her mind screamed, "Excited! Excited? How could I be excited? You have dragged me away from friends, and family, to this hateful place, and now you want me to leave to travel thousands of miles to the other side of this strange land where we know no one?!?!" But her voice said, "Of course, dear."

The next afternoon they bid Father O'Malley farewell and thanked him for his help and hospitality. Then they boarded the train. The second leg of their journey to a new life was about to begin.

The trip from Montréal to Kamloops was uneventful, except for the fact that Liam's condition worsened. His cough grew more insistent and he began to lose weight. This worried Caitlin, but she continued to administer the cough medicine and dismissed his weight loss as a normal thing that happens when children get sick.

As the train pulled into the valley where Kamloops was nestled, Caitlin looked out the window to see their adopted homeland. What she saw made her breath catch in her throat; naked, jagged mountains thrust themselves against the open sky. The yellow, dusty valley was barren; the only thing that gave the steep valley any sign of life was the Thompson

River, which sliced the valley in two like a blue-green snake. Caitlin wondered why they had left their soft, lush hills for this foreboding, desolate landscape.

There was no Father O'Malley to greet them when they arrived in the very western setting of Kamloops, as they had heard tell of back home.

Looking out of the taxicab's window, Liam saw the citizens' attire and excitedly exclaimed, "Look at the cowboys! Aidan and Rory were right! But where are all the Indians?" The cabdriver responded that there would be plenty of Indians to see when the powwow came to town in the summer.

The cabby helped them unload their boxes onto the sidewalk in front of the apartment complex where they were to live. The tall, narrow, three-storey walk-up building was not in the best of shape. The white stucco walls had grown dingy over years of neglect; the roof was missing shingles, the front door's brown paint was chipped and the broken glass panels were held together by tape.

Surrounded by their luggage, Caitlin looked up to see people peering out at them from beneath their curtains. She smiled up at them, but only one woman smiled back. Shamus had already begun to bring the heavier boxes into their apartment. Caitlin started to pick up a box, but Shamus took it from her saying, "My dear, you shouldn't be carrying heavy things in your condition."

"What am I supposed to do, then, Shamus? I'm not completely incapable, for goodness sakes. I'm only seven-months pregnant!" she cried, her Irish temper flaring up.

Shamus just smiled and told her, "Why don't you go in, darling, and start to unpack."

She stomped her foot angrily, but went inside anyway, being curious as to what her new home would look like.

Caitlin was pleasantly surprised at their first floor apartment. A quick investigation showed two small bedrooms furnished with a bed, desk and dresser each. A small kitchen was equipped with a functioning stove, fridge, a full bank of cupboards and a cheap table and chair set. Much to her delight she discovered their own tidy little bathroom. The living room, although small, like everything else in the house, was warm and cozy. The floors were carpeted, the couch set was in good repair and a few pictures hung on the walls. It wasn't as nice as their home back in Dungannon, but it was acceptable.

As the O'Connors were unpacking, they heard a knock at the door. Caitlin opened the door and saw the woman that had smiled at her from the window. This black-haired, blue-eyed woman introduced herself with a smile.

"Hi, I'm Connie Johnston. I saw you come in this morning, and I just couldn't wait to come and meet you! I live upstairs in #2B. Mind if I come in?" She entered the small apartment with gifts in hand, a loaf of bread and a bag of salt, "For wishes of food at the table always, and prosperity," she said.

The next morning, Liam looked out the window and saw a group of children playing just outside the building. He ran to his parents and asked, "Mum, Da, can I go out to play with those kids?"

Caitlin looked worried, but said, "Of course you can darling, but are you sure you're feeling well enough?"

"Of course I am, Mum!" he replied.

"Then run along little man!" Shamus said. He and Caitlin both smiled as their boy ran happily out the door.

Minutes later Liam burst inside, crying, his face and clothes covered in mud. Through his tears he said, "They made fun of me because of the way I talk, and made me come home!"

"And why are you covered in mud?" Caitlin asked quietly.

"When I was walking away, one of the big kids pushed me down into the mud, and everybody laughed!" Liam told her, bursting into tears again.

Caitlin held him in her arms and said, "It'll be all right, don't worry, my baby." Over Liam's head, Caitlin looked at her husband with anguished eyes.

Later, some of the neighbours came to her door to tell her to keep her sick child away from theirs. Her spirits fell as she realized that Connie was to be her only friend in the building.

Her spirits were buoyed as she remembered that they still had to attend church. At church, her spirits were once again crushed, as her family was forced to sit at the back of the church, even though there were plenty of spaces available closer to the front. Their clothes were very different from to the rest of the churchgoers, making her family stick out like a sore thumb. She could feel people glaring at them whenever Liam coughed. As they sang and as they went up to receive the Host, she felt eyes burning holes in her back.

At the end of the service, Father Rhems, the priest who performed the ceremony, came up to them and said; "You must be the O'Connors. Father O'Malley has told me so much about you. I hope the housing set up is suitable. And if you need anything else, don't hesitate to ask."

Shamus thanked him and the O'Connor family left for home.

Shamus left a week later, Father Rhems having arranged for him to work in a logging camp up the Thompson River. Caitlin was distressed to learn that he would be gone for months at a time, since coming home on his few days off would cost too much.

That night she confided, "Shamus, I'm afraid to be alone here. What will happen when it's time?" She took his large hand and placed it on her ripening belly.

Holding her in his arms, he promised her that everything would work out. He would make enough money to support them and he would come back as often as he could.

Caitlin received Shamus's first paycheck a few weeks after he left. As soon as she received it, she realized it would not cover rent, and food costs, taxes, and Liam's schooling for next year; plus, Liam's condition had worsened. His breathing was now raspy, and he complained of chest pain. He had lost even more weight and always seemed to have a temperature. Caitlin knew that she needed to get him to a doctor, but with this small amount of money how could she?

That day, Connie came down for a visit. She found Caitlin sitting at the kitchen table, muttering angrily as she divided the money. "What's wrong, Caitlin?" Connie asked quietly.

"We don't have enough money to pay the rent, get food, pay the taxes, pay for Liam's schooling next year and bring him to the doctor!" Caitlin cried.

"Caitlin, you don't need to pay to take Liam to the doctor, or pay for his schooling," Connie said gently. "We have a healthcare and an educational system here. And about the money, I can help you out, or, you could get a job."

Caitlin was a proud woman. She kindly refused to take any money, but she was intrigued by the possibility of work. Connie told her she knew of an opening at the nearby laundry facility.

That night, as she lay awake listening to Liam cough in the next room and feeling her baby tossing in her stomach, she thought, "Shamus was right, Canada does have some amazing possibilities. At least I can give my children a fighting chance. Liam won't be sick so often, because I can take him to the doctor for free. Our children will have a good future because they will have a good, solid, education...."

With this glimmer of hope, she fell asleep with a smile on her face; the grudge that she had clung on to for so long had been resolved. Canada was no longer her sworn enemy.

The next day, Tuesday, she awoke, feeling like her old self again:

strong, confident, and proud. She and Liam walked down to the laundry facility, which was situated next-door to the provincial sanatorium, "Tranquille". At first, the managers were hesitant to give a pregnant woman even a short-term job. They were even more reluctant when they found out that Liam would have to accompany her. But, despite all this, Caitlin received the job.

"After all," one of the managers said to the other, "the Irish are good, hard workers."

Leaving the facility, Caitlin and Liam headed toward the spire of Saint Joseph's with a joyful bounce in their step. At church, she walked up the aisle with Liam to a pew closer to the front and sat down. The man sitting next to her turned, startled and said, "Hey you! You and your kind don't belong here!"

She turned. Her steely gray eyes flashing, she looked him straight in the eye and said icily, "How dare you! What right do you have to treat us like this, in a house of God no less?"

The man's mouth dropped. This was not the reaction he had been expecting. Caitlin's buttermilk skin flushed with victory as she turned to face the altar, a slight smile on her lips, as the adrenaline pulsed through her body, causing her to tremble.

Leaving the church, Caitlin returned all the glares she received with an equally cold, hard stare. She then turned up the street to take Liam to the nearest doctor, her legs shaking, but with a smile on her face.

After examining him, the doctor took Caitlin into the next room. Doctor Brown looked at her squarely and asked, "Within the past year, did he have any contact with someone who suffered from similar symptoms?"

Caitlin's mind raced, then she remembered, "Grandfather McLaugh! He died on the ship. Oh God!" she blurted out.

"He shows clear signs of tuberculosis. Did he not get his BCG vaccine as an infant?" Doctor Brown asked gravely.

"No, we couldn't afford it. Tuberculosis? Are you sure?" Caitlin demanded, aghast. She had heard of this infectious disease. As her thoughts raced, she asked, "How? Is there anything to do? Will he die?" The last question stuck in her throat, as if saying it made it so.

The doctor muttered, "I'm surprised they let you in with such a sick child," but said out loud, "I'm afraid that we have to send your son to Tranquille immediately. Don't worry though, you will be allowed to visit him."

Five minutes later, Liam was taken to the sanatorium.

Life got harder for Caitlin with Liam's confinement. When she wasn't working, she was with him at his sickbed. Her back and feet ached from being bent over the hot wash tubs in her condition. Her hands were red and cracking from working in the laundry. And then, on his third day in the sanatorium, Liam's condition took a grave turn. His fever rose to the point of delirium, and he began to cough up blood. He began to babble, strangely twisting the events of the past months. Between shifts Caitlin tended to her son, sponging him down to try and relieve his fever, murmuring into his ear his favorite stories and songs.

Through his delirium, Liam opened his eyes, looked at his mother and said, "Sing me my lullaby, Mum."

Caitlin knew which one it was, even though she had not sung "The Gartan Mother's Lullaby" to him since he was a toddler. Lying beside him, stroking his damp head gently, her soft, clear voice rang out in a melody filled with love.

"Sleep, O babe, for the red bee hums
The silent twilight fall.
The Banshee from the grey rocks comes
To wrap the earth in thrall.
My baby-o, my child, my joy,
My love, my heart's desire,
The cricket sings you lullaby,
Beside the dying fire.

"Dusk is drawn, and the Green Man's thorn
Is wreathed in rings of fog.
The fairy sails his boat til morn,
Upon the starry bog.
My child-o, the pale half moon
Hath brimmed her cusp in dew,
And weeps to hear this sad sleep tune,
I sing, my love, to you..."

Occasionally, throughout the song, Caitlin could hear Liam's wee voice singing along with her, causing her throat to tighten. As they finished the lullaby, Liam closed his eyes contentedly. Caitlin kissed his damp forehead and got up to get some more water to sponge him down. As she filled the basin he weakly called out, "Mum." She rushed to him, but he was gone. Her first born was dead.

Overcome with grief and guilt, she grew hysterical. She picked up his limp body and ran out of the sanatorium, past the guards, out into the streets, tears streaming down her face and began screaming, "I'm sorry, I'm sorry! Oh God, help us! Won't somebody please help us?"

But no one came; she began to run, not knowing where she was going. Her hair, which had fallen from its neat braid, streamed behind her. Her feet carried her to the church. She ran inside, laid her son's limp body on the altar steps, and screamed, "Father please help us. Pray for my son!" She knelt, cupped her head in her hands, and prayed.

Father Rhems rushed in, and taking in the scene, called to a nun, "Sister, call an ambulance." As the nun hurried away, he reached Liam, and realized he was gone. Father Rhems performed the Last Rites, crossing over the little forehead, lips, and heart. He then went to comfort Caitlin.

"My child, what happened?" he asked.

She stood up and hysterically told the story of the trip, the comments, the bullies, the hatred, the pain, and the fear, which was so jumbled Father Rhems could make nothing of it. She stopped suddenly, as she felt a wetness between her legs and the overwhelming spasms of childbirth. She collapsed onto the floor clutching her stomach.

The ambulance arrived just in time to deliver her baby girl right there in the church. Although weak from the quick, painful birth, Caitlin insisted on having her baptized, fearing her child would die. Caitlin turned to Father Rhems and said, "Father, give my baby a proper Canadian name."

Father Rhems contemplated this question for a few moments before he answered decisively, "Molly. It's both Canadian and Irish." After the baptism, both Caitlin and Molly were immediately taken to the hospital. Miraculously, both of them survived.

Liam's funeral was small, but sorrowful. Shamus had been able to make it back to Kamloops for the funeral, but would have to leave almost immediately afterwards. Although he was excited about the arrival of his new daughter, the grief of losing his first son weighed heavily on his heart. He and Caitlin clung to each other, weeping openly, as Liam's small coffin was placed into the ground. Caitlin was surprised and comforted to see that a few people from the building and church came to pay their respects.

After the funeral and Shamus's all too soon departure, Caitlin and Molly were left alone. Caitlin sat in a rocking chair with her small, rosy baby cradled in her arms. Her eyes wandered around the room and fell on a colourful sheet of cowboys and Indians that Liam had drawn on the ship. As a storm of memories arose, she looked down into Molly's baby blue eyes, and vowed, "Molly, I promise to make your life in Canada the very best possible."

MADD About You

Lindsay Chung

Smoke rose from the engine of a dark blue Honda Accord, and the smell of burning rubber hung in the air. As a torrent of rain poured down, muffled cries could be heard coming from the car. Other cars driving along the highway pulled over, and men and women ran toward the Accord and a white Toyota Tercel, crushed together in a heap, and a black Ford Escort flipped on its right side in the ditch. The busy highway was a tangle of steel and glass, and people came rushing toward the scene of the terrible accident.

"If anyone can hear me, don't move!" someone yelled, eyes wide with amazement. People came from all directions, attracted by the smoke, scattered car parts and the horrific noise they had heard seconds earlier.

In the driver's seat of the Escort, Marilyn sat sideways, restrained only by her seatbelt. Her blue eyes were clouded over in confusion, and her heart was pounding with the force of a thousand men breaking down a heavy door. As Marilyn closed her eyes, she heard the sloshing sound of feet pounding on the puddle-strewn pavement.

A man gasped as he came to the overturned Escort. The front end was a crumpled mess of steel and broken headlights, and the passenger's side door had caved in, trapping the young male inside.

As a young woman crawled over to check out the passenger's side, she was horrified to see a teenage boy lying there, crumpled and unconscious. Blood poured from a deep wound in his head, and he barely looked human.

A group of men and women worked carefully to extract Marilyn from the car. She burst into tears as she began to realise where she was. She shivered from the cold, rain mixing with the tears streaming down her cheeks.

"Ryan?!" she screamed, "How's Ryan?"

Marilyn felt a blanket being wrapped around her, and she could hear people trying frantically to calm her down.

The autumn storm picked up, and the wind threw broken pieces of the Ford's side mirrors along the side of the road. Marilyn saw the damaged door hanging from her Escort and watched it sway in the fierce wind.

Meanwhile, another group of people had gathered around the Honda Accord. Pieces of red glass were scattered along the highway, and the back end of this car was ruined. As men and women approached the car, they heard Berlin's hit song "Take my Breath Away" playing loudly from the radio.

Opening the driver's side door, a man found a middle-aged woman slumped over the steering wheel, dazed but still conscious. As he bent to check the woman's breathing, the man could detect the pungent odor of whiskey. He sighed, disgusted, as he continued checking her over. She did not seem to have any major injuries, and there was no one else in the car with her.

Another group of people were attending to the young woman sitting unconscious in the Tercel, her head pressed against the dashboard. Wind whipped through the car's open door, and pieces of paper swirled fiercely out into the rain

As Marilyn stood there in the rain and wind, a trickle of blood dripped down her face; but she was oblivious to the liquid coursing along her cold skin. She did not recognize any of the men and women talking to her and could not hear the words they cried as they asked her questions. Lost in her own whirlwind of emotion, Marilyn ignored them. She heard the loud noises of ambulance and police sirens. In the distance, obscured by the pouring rain, she could almost make out the shape of an ambulance heading toward them.

The smell of hospitals always made Marilyn uneasy; and as she sat in the emergency room, she held her blanket closer to her shivering body. As doctors and nurses rushed past, she remembered the crushing sound of the cars hitting each other as the Accord tried to pass her but hit the front end of her Escort instead. She grimaced, remembering how the force had caused her to lose control of her car. On the slick road, the Escort swerved and spun, the sound of screeching tires drowning out the radio; and they eventually landed in a ditch, the Escort lying on its side. She recalled the piercing sound of her screams, and she remembered looking over at Ryan and seeing his big blue eyes wide open in terror. It all happened in a split second but took a lifetime.

Marilyn started crying again. The nurses brought her up to the children's ward to await the results of Ryan's operation. She looked around, blue eyes wide with shock, and saw all of the children crying. She saw the grim, scared faces of others in her position.

As the night wore on, someone bandaged Marilyn's head and gave her a strong sleeping pill. Sitting in a brown plastic chair, she fell asleep.

A few hours later, Marilyn awoke, unable to recall where she was. As she wearily rubbed her eyes and looked up, she was surprised to see a tall, white-haired doctor looking down at her. Her heart skipped a beat when she saw his serious expression and sad, brown eyes.

"Mrs. Taylor? I am Dr. Bradley Smith. I'm very grieved to inform you that, despite our best efforts, your son Ryan James Taylor has succumbed to his injuries."

Marilyn gasped, her eyes filling with tears as she remembered where she was.

"In the accident, he sustained massive head injuries and injuries to his internal organs which were too serious to repair. We tried our best, but his numerous injuries were just too much, even for our expert staff. I'm terribly sorry, Mrs. Taylor."

Marilyn stared up at the doctor, replaying his words in her head. Her slender fingers turned white as her grip tightened around her blanket, unconsciously twisting it in distress.

"Ryan's dead..." she whispered sadly, tears rolling down her pale cheeks.

"Are you going to be okay, Mrs. Taylor?" Dr. Smith asked, concern wrinkling his forehead. "We were unable to reach your husband Jack, so we've called your sister. Anne is going to come by to pick you up, and she will take you home. Is that alright?"

"Ryan's dead..." Marilyn rose uncertainly when she saw Anne running toward her.

Anne opened the apartment and followed Marilyn in. Once in her apartment, Marilyn sank to the floor, sobbing. "Ohh.... My baby...." Anne stood back, moved by the sight of her younger sister crying on the cold floor. Through her tears, Marilyn saw Ryan's large school graduation picture hanging on the wall behind the black leather couch. She buried her head in her hands, unable to withstand the wave of grief that washed over her. Her body shook, and the living room blurred through her watery vision.

Anne too began to weep, her initial shock wearing off. She knelt down and wrapped her long arms around Marilyn's trembling body.

An hour later, when she had calmed down, Marilyn called her husband on his cell phone.

"Hello?" a deep, weary voice answered the phone.

"Jack," Marilyn cried breathlessly, "can you come home right now? It's very important."

"Marilyn, I'm at the airport right now. I still have to pick up my luggage, so I will still be quite a while." Jack answered, rather impatiently.

"But Jack, you have to come home." Her voice broke, and Marilyn took a deep breath. "Ryan and I were in an accident." She started to cry and felt Anne's warm hand enclose her own.

"What? Are you okay? What happened?"

Marilyn continued crying, unable to speak.

"Get a grip on yourself! What happened? Are you okay? Stop crying and answer me!"

"Please come home," Marilyn said softly through her tears, "it's important."

"I'll be there as soon as I can," Jack said, slamming the phone down.

Marilyn held the receiver in her trembling hand, listening to the silence. Her slim body shook as large tears flowed down her face. After a few minutes, she replaced the receiver and smoothed her long, brown hair out of her face. She looked into her sister's large hazel eyes.

"You should get home to your kids," she said softly, "I'll be okay. Don't worry."

Promising to return the next day, Anne hugged Marilyn tightly. She left, looking sadly over her shoulder as she closed the door behind her.

Half an hour later, Jack stormed into the apartment, his light brown eyes flashing. He stood in the middle of the living room. "Okay Marilyn, tell me what happened."

Marilyn ran to her husband of eighteen years, still clothed in her rain-soaked garments and covered in her blanket.

Jack grabbed her shoulders with his strong arms. "What happened to your head? Where's Ryan?"

"We were driving home on the highway." Marilyn's voice shook and her thin lips trembled as she spoke. "And it was stormy and cold." She started shaking as she looked down at the plush white carpet. "A car tried to pass us, but it braked, and..."

"And?" Jack asked, his light brown eyes searching Marilyn's wet, blue ones.

"And, the Escort rammed into its back end. The vehicle started to spin and swerve, and I couldn't stop it. I tried so hard; I was pulling the steering wheel with all of my strength, but I just couldn't stop it." She looked up at her husband, afraid to continue. Taking a deep breath, Marilyn spoke again, "The Escort rolled onto its side. Ryan was on the bottom, and , and... We went to the hospital." A sob escaped her throat. "Ryan's dead," she whispered.

Marilyn felt Jack's hands tighten around her shoulders and then loosen. He swept a large hand over his eyes, his breathing becoming shallower as he found it harder to get air.

"He's dead? Ryan? Ryan's dead?"

All Marilyn could do was nod, her tears falling onto the carpet.

Jack stood, dumbfounded, looking around the living room but not seeing anything. In his mind, he pictured the day before when he and Ryan had been throwing a baseball around in the yard. He remembered how he had looked at Ryan and realised how old he was. His seventeen year old son would be going off to college next year... Jack turned and walked into the kitchen. Not now... Ryan would never get to go to college.

Jack poured himself a scotch and drank it back in one gulp. He twirled his empty glass in his hand. Ryan would never play baseball again, would never go out with his friends, would never learn to drive. All of a sudden, Jack threw his empty glass down on the linoleum floor. The glass broke into little pieces that scattered around the kitchen like exploding fireworks. Tears came to his eyes, and he rushed into the bedroom, slamming the door behind him.

Marilyn jumped at the loud noise. As Jack mourned in their bedroom, she went to the kitchen. Pulling her blanket close to her, Marilyn kneeled down and slowly began to pick up the pieces of broken glass. Tears poured from her eyes as she heard muffled sobs coming from the bedroom.

"It wasn't my fault, " she whispered softly, "I didn't do anything wrong..."

***

Five months later, Marilyn sat on the black leather couch, idly flipping through her book. Restless, she got up and pushed aside the white curtains. Looking out at the snow covered lawn, tears came to Marilyn's eyes. The last two months had been very difficult for her and her family.

The door opened, and Jack walked in. He came over and kissed Marilyn mechanically on the cheek. "I got a lot of work done today," he said, walking to the kitchen to pour himself a whiskey, "that lady will definitely pay for what she did."

Marilyn stared at her husband as he polished off his second glass of whiskey. She sighed, worried. She noticed that his skin was pale and that there were dark circles under his eyes. She knew that these last few months had been especially hard for Jack. He had taken on the job of helping to prosecute the woman who had hit them that night in September. Marilyn wrapped her arms around herself and sighed again. The woman had been drunk when she had hit them and was facing hefty fines and a possible jail sentence.

Marilyn didn't know why Jack had agreed to take this job. It was ruining him. She knew that Jack wanted to put that woman away, but was it really worth it? Jack was constantly working, he was pale and tired, and he was drinking more than he ever had. Marilyn stared across the room at her husband, whose back was turned to her. Worst of all, he barely spent any time at home anymore. Long nights of work kept him away; and by the time he came home at night, she was already asleep.

"Honey, I'm going to go for a walk. Do you want to come?" Marilyn asked, pulling on her snow boots and winter jacket.

"No, I've still got a lot of work to do." Jack didn't even turn around.

Marilyn pulled her scarf over her face, trying to hide the tears that came to her eyes. She walked out the door and headed down the stairs.

Once outside her apartment building, Marilyn took a deep breath of the cool, February air. It was three o'clock, and the sun was still shining as she walked quickly down the street toward Granville Island. The cool air brought a touch of pink to Marilyn's cheeks, and she forgot about all of her grief and hurt for a minute. She remembered when Ryan was a little boy and how happy they had all been. They had been such a close family, always cheerful and optimistic.

She remembered the times before Ryan had been born. She and Jack hadn't had any problems being alone together then. Life had been wonderful. She looked up at the setting sun. "It's amazing how much things change," she whispered quietly to herself as she walked around Granville Island, her hands pushed into her pockets.

When she got to the doorstep of her apartment building half an hour later, Marilyn sat down. She noticed the pile of newspapers lying there, and she picked them up. She noticed a bright black and red pamphlet tucked in with the papers.

"MADD," she read, " refers to Mothers Against Drunk Driving." Marilyn shivered. Why did she get this pamphlet? Did everyone know about Ryan's death? Was it that obvious that she was a mother whose son had been killed? Marilyn continued to read the pamphlet, unable to tear her eyes away from it. She read that the women of MADD were desperately looking for help to put together a booth for Expo. The ad was asking for any capable women to help them, saying that the experience would be worthwhile. Marilyn's mind spun in turmoil as she thought about what she had just read. She knew that she should get out and do something to get her mind off of her grief, but she shuddered at the thought of going out into the world again. It was too soon; she wasn't ready. How could she possibly help that group of women when she couldn't even help herself?

"I can't do it," she told herself softly, "I can't help them. I don't know how to."

Marilyn ran her mittened hand over her hair as tears welled up in her eyes. Her breath came out as a cloud in the winter's air as she sighed and stood up. She fumbled in the late afternoon darkness to unlock the door. Inside, she went upstairs to her apartment, eager to relax and forget about MADD.

Jack was not home when Marilyn got in. Not surprised, she heated up some left-overs for herself. When she was finished eating, Marilyn had a bath.

Done with her bath and in her pajamas, Marilyn went into the living room. She walked over to the bookshelf beside the television. She ran her slender fingers along the well-worn broken spines of her books, finally selecting her bent copy of You Can Heal Your Life by Louise L. Hay. Taking her book and a cup of tea, Marilyn settled into bed. She read for a few hours by the light of her bedside lamp before falling into a restless sleep.

For the next couple of days, Marilyn couldn't get MADD out of her mind. She read the pamphlet over and over, each time shuddering with the realisation that she was one of them. She was a mother whose son had been killed by a drunk driver. That was her reality, and nothing was going to change that. Marilyn went around the house in a daze, barely eating and reading her self-help books like crazy.

One night, she was astonished to see Jack come home from work early. He brought her a bottle of wine and Chinese food takeout.

"I'm surprised to see you here for dinner," Marilyn said, standing on her tip toes to kiss Jack on the cheek.

"I decided I'd done enough work for the day. We still don't have a trial date set for that woman." Jack sighed as he went to the kitchen to get some plates.

Marilyn set the kitchen table and watched as Jack poured two glasses of wine. He turned on the radio, and the songs of Bryan Adams and Whitney Houston filled the air. As Jack and Marilyn ate their food, they were quiet for a while.

"How was your day?" Jack asked, biting into his egg roll.

"Pretty good, thanks."

Jack glanced at Marilyn and then at the tattered copy of How to Survive the Loss of a Love lying on the coffee table.

"Well, I got a new case today. I'm prosecuting a man who broke into an elderly lady's house and robbed her. This should go on without a hitch."

"That's good," Marilyn said, taking a sip of her drink.

Jack poured himself another glass of wine and helped himself to more fried rice. "Gee, we're pretty lucky; the weather has been really nice. Ryan would have-" he stopped, amazed at his slip.

Marilyn looked up from her half-eaten chop suey. They stared at each other for a minute, uncertain, not even hearing the music coming from the radio.

"Well, we hired a new paralegal. He's twenty two years old and very bright. I think it's going to work out well," he said, his tone a little over-enthusiastic to make up for the awkward silence.

"That's good." Marilyn pushed her food around, unable to eat.

While neither of them talked, the radio droned songs by Micheal Jackson and Z.Z. Top.

"So. " Jack pulled the familiar red and black pamphlet out of his pocket. "I found this in the living room last night. What are you doing?"

"Nothing. I read where this group called MADD was looking for help to design a booth for Expo."

"And how much money would you have to give them?" Jack asked coldly.

"The pamphlet does not mention money."

"Right. So why don't you help these women? You could all sit around, compare sad stories and get each other's sympathy," Jack said sarcastically, finishing yet another glass of wine.

"That's not fair," Marilyn cried, glaring at Jack, "it's not like that!

It's a good group."

Jack pounded his fist on the table. "It's just a scam."

Marilyn stood up, tears in her eyes. "No, it's not! Don't you understand? Helping them design the booth could help me." She rushed out of the room and slammed the bedroom door behind her.

Jack finished off the bottle of wine. He crumpled the MADD pamphlet up in his hand. "We don't need help," he whispered, closing his eyes.

For the next two weeks, life continued its empty pace for Marilyn. She didn't see Jack very often, as he spent a lot of time at the law office. Marilyn spent most of her time alone, thinking. Her mind filled with thoughts, ideas and questions. Every night she would lie in her cold, empty bed before Jack came home and ask herself why she was put on this earth. What was her purpose in life? Did she matter at all in the grand scheme of things?

Marilyn spent a lot of this time thinking about MADD. She had recovered the pamphlet, even though she had memorised every word of it. Marilyn began to seriously consider the request for help to build a booth for Expo. Perhaps it really would help her. Many people had told her that an important step in recovery was to get involved in something, and this did seem like a good project to become involved in. Marilyn started reading up on MADD and what kind of things they did.

One night, unable to sleep for more than an hour at a time, Marilyn decided, once and for all, that she would help the ladies at MADD design a booth for Expo. She sat up and blinked, her eyes still adjusting to the dark. Marilyn pulled her comforter in to her chin, and she saw Jack lying next to her, sleeping quietly with his back toward her. She saw the rigid lines of his shoulders through his thin grey t-shirt and sighed. She didn't know what to do about him. Marilyn knew that Jack would never agree to therapy, and besides, he was too busy. But maybe she could have her own therapy and then be able to help Jack. Perhaps working on the booth would be therapeutic for her.

After breakfast, Marilyn had a hot shower. If she was going to turn her life around, she wanted to be clean and refreshed.

She stood by the telephone for five minutes, holding the pamphlet containing Joanne Olson's phone number in her trembling hand, a little nervous about making the phone call. Marilyn took a deep breath and dialed the number.

"Hello?" a soft, feminine voice answered.

"Hi, is this Joanne Olson?"

"Yes it is." Marilyn was relieved to hear the cheerful sound of the woman's voice.

"I received a pamphlet about MADD in the mail two weeks ago, and I read that you need help designing a booth for the upcoming Expo."

"Yes that's true." Joanne coughed. "Do you know much about Mothers Against Drunk Driving?"

Marilyn bit her lip softly, slightly embarrassed. "Not too much, I'm afraid. Only what I've read in the pamphlet and in the newspaper."

"Well, Marilyn, our non-profit organisation has been in existence since 1980, and our mission is to stop drunk driving and to support victims of this crime."

"That's great. I, well..." Marilyn gulped, feeling a large lump forming in her throat. "My son died in September from a drunk driver," she said, tears coming to her eyes.

"I'm so sorry, Marilyn."

"Oh, thank you. I was calling because I'd like to help you with your booth, but I don't know what I can do."

"Oh, we could definitely find something for you to do. If you'd like to come, Marilyn, we are going to work on it today at four o'clock. Our booth is in my garage right now. It's not much, but we've got some great ideas." Marilyn could hear the excitement and pride in Joanne's voice, and she felt optimistic about her decision.

"I'm sure you do. I'll be there at four o'clock."

"That's great. Marilyn, I'm so glad that you'll be with us," Joanne said as she gave Marilyn an address in the West End.

"So, I'll see you there," Marilyn said, pleased.

"Okay, goodbye," Joanne said cheerfully as she hung up.

Marilyn hung up the phone and smiled, satisfied. She had done something good for herself. "That's a start," she told herself as she poured a glass of orange juice.

From then until four o'clock, Marilyn was jumpy, her nerves on edge. Marilyn tried to read another of her books, but she couldn't concentrate.

Jack amazed Marilyn when he came home for lunch, and they ate sandwiches together.

"So how has work been?" Marilyn asked, unsure of whether to tell him about her choice or not, as she remembered his outburst when he found the pamphlet.

"Oh, not too badly. We aren't getting anywhere with that drunk woman's case though." He looked at his wife. "But don't worry; we'll get her one day. She'll pay for what she did to us."

Marilyn chewed thoughtfully on her sandwich. No one could

pay for that.

"I'm doing a lot of work on my robbery case. I probably won't be home 'till late tonight," Jack said.

"That's okay. I'll leave you some left-overs."

"Thanks."

When Jack left, Marilyn shook her head thoughtfully. Jack had been so decent today, not as cold as usual. Marilyn had also noticed that he hadn't had one drink with lunch. She smiled. Maybe this really was the start of better times.

At a quarter to four, Marilyn got into her new white Buick. She drove to Joanne's house, still a little nervous.

When she got out of her car, Marilyn was greeted instantly by Joanne.

"Marilyn! I'm so glad you could come. I'd like you to meet Cindy," Joanne said, smiling brightly as she gestured toward a young, blonde woman.

The three women walked toward the garage and went inside.

"This is Linda," Cindy said, pointing to a short woman in her late forties.

"And this is Diane," Joanne said, pointing to a plump woman in her thirties.

"Hi, I'm Maria," a tall woman in her forties said, "and this is Karen," she said, pointing to the tall woman beside her.

"It's nice to meet you," Marilyn said, shaking every woman's hand.

"Well, ladies," Joanne said as she brought out a fairly large wooden booth, "this is what we have so far. Now, I was thinking that we could make a really large red and white banner saying MADD and hang it over the top."

The women all nodded.

"That sounds good," Linda said.

They sat around, bouncing ideas off one another for an hour. After that, they all went across the street to the cafe and sat around a large table, drinking coffee and tea for another half an hour.

Marilyn laughed and smiled more in that hour and a half than she had in the five and a half months since Ryan's death. The light sounds of the other women's laughter rang in Marilyn's ears, and she felt warm and secure in their company. The cafe was warm and light, and Marilyn really enjoyed herself in the pleasant environment.

As she drove home along Granville Street, Marilyn was happy that she had gone.

When she got to her apartment, Marilyn made herself some spaghetti. She sat at the table, thinking up some more ideas for the booth as she twirled the noodles around her fork.

That night, Marilyn finally slept well without waking up in the middle of the night in a cold sweat. She felt peaceful; and when she awoke, Marilyn felt fresh and invigorated.

Marilyn made herself some breakfast and looked over the schedule she had been given the night before. They were going to work on the booth every Monday afternoon for an hour at three o'clock.

For the next few months, Marilyn went to every MADD booth-building session. She put all of her energy into creating an attractive and eye-catching booth. Marilyn became more and more excited about her work and began to feel more hopeful.

One day as Marilyn was painting a sign for the booth, Joanne came and sat beside her.

"Marilyn, how are you today?"

"I'm pretty well thanks. How are you?"

"Not bad at all. I won't waste any of your time, Marilyn. As you know, Maria has been in charge of decorations for our booth these last couple of months. I have a problem now. Maria has to fly home to Alberta and take care of her mother. So, I need someone else to be in charge of decorations."

"I'll do it," Marilyn said, the excitement obvious in her voice, "I mean, if you want me to."

"I do want you to; that's why I brought it up." Joanne smiled at Marilyn and hugged her. "Thanks Marilyn."

"Thank you Joanne."

Joanne left, and Marilyn continued her painting, a wide smile spread across her face.

As the weeks passed, Marilyn became increasingly busy with the booth. She was out looking for ideas for the project almost every day. Healthy color came to Marilyn's skin; and with more sleep, she had more energy. Marilyn started cooking more; and as a result, Jack came home for dinner more often. He was still very busy at work, but he made an effort to come home more. When Jack came home, he was more pleasant, even though he did have his moments of weakness. Marilyn was pleased to see that Jack was drinking less. Things were looking up for them, and Marilyn felt happier.

With her new responsibility with MADD, Marilyn started feeling better about herself. She found it hard because she missed Ryan so much, but the heavy weight on her heart was lifting. Marilyn told herself that if she could help just one person with her work, it would be worth it. Perhaps, she was put on the earth for a special reason. Maybe this was it. Maybe she was here to help other people.

Finally, a couple of weeks before the official opening of Expo, the booth was finished. Marilyn stood back and admired the bright red paint on the signs and the sparkles adorning the booth.

"It's really good," Cindy said, putting her arm around Marilyn's shoulders. "I'm proud; I think we did a great job."

Marilyn smiled. "Yah, it looks really good."

"Let's go to the cafe," Joanne said, and the women all headed over to the cafe and took their usual table.

"You know," Linda said, sipping her tea, "we should have a party to celebrate."

"That's a great idea," Joanne said, assuming her usual leadership role. "It's Monday now; how about we have our party on Saturday?"

"Saturday's good," one by one, the women agreed.

That night, Marilyn went to bed, happy and proud of her accomplishment. She felt excited about the upcoming Expo and was proud to be a part of MADD.

A week later, Marilyn drove to Joanne's house. As she entered the sprawling brick house, Marilyn looked around and smiled happily. She took off her rain jacket and carried her plate of homemade cookies into the kitchen.

"Marilyn!" Karen cried, coming up to her. Spirits were high, and the radio was on, playing the songs of The Cars and Bob Marley, as the women gathered to celebrate their achievement. The large living room was lively with many happy people and two little poodles.

"Here's to us! Yesterday, I moved our booth to Canada Place, where it will be until Expo is over. We're done!" Joanne cried, lifting her glass of water. Everyone clinked their glasses together and cheered. "Hooray!"

For the next two hours, Marilyn sat, talked, danced and laughed, enjoying herself thoroughly. When she took her jacket to leave, Marilyn hugged everyone.

"Thank you everybody. I had a wonderful time doing this booth. It was a lot of fun, and it helped me very much." Marilyn said, smiling brightly.

"Thank you for all of your hard work." Joanne smiled happily. "We'll call you if we need to do anything more."

"Okay, I'll see you later." Marilyn walked out to her car and drove home.

When she got into the apartment, Marilyn was surprised to see Jack. He was not usually home at this time.

"Hi." She smiled. "How was work?"

"Pretty good. Where were you?" Jack asked, surprised that his wife had not been home when he arrived.

"Well-"

Suddenly, the sound of the telephone startled Marilyn, and she walked over to answer it.

"Hello?" she asked.

"Hi, Marilyn? This is Joanne." She sounded really upset. "I just got a phone call from the night guards at Canada Place. They just told me that a group of teenagers broke into the building and vandalised all the booths. I don't know what to do."

"Vandalised? They ruined our booth?" Marilyn stood, shocked. "But, we just finished it; that's not fair."

"I know," Joanne said, distress evident in the tone of her voice.

"Well, thanks for telling me. Expo is only a few weeks away; what are we going to do?"

" I guess we'll just sleep on it and do something tomorrow." Joanne sighed. "Try to have a good sleep, Marilyn."

"You too, Joanne."

Marilyn hung up, stunned and upset. She turned around, her hands shaking.

Jack stared at her. "What was that all about?"

Marilyn started to cry. "Our booth for Expo was vandalised. It's ruined." Her voice shook. "We worked so hard on it."

"Your booth?" Jack swept a piece of black hair from Marilyn's eyes. "You've been working on a booth this whole time?"

"Yes." Marilyn shook with the power of her sobs. "Remember MADD? Well, I've been helping them for a few months. I was even in charge of decorations."

Jack wrapped his arms around Marilyn.

"I'm sorry," he whispered.

She rested her head on Jack's broad chest for a second. She breathed in deeply. How she missed being held by him.

"I'm going to go to Canada Place. Maybe I can salvage some things."

Tears streaming down her face, Marilyn grabbed her purple jacket and ran to the door.

"Marilyn!"

Her hand gripping the doorknob tightly, Marilyn turned around. She swept a trail of tears from her cheek as she looked at her husband.

"I'll be home in a little while," she said, walking out the door and closing it softly behind her.

As she drove to Canada Place, Marilyn pictured her beautiful booth torn down and broken, its bright paint scratched off. The project she had worked so hard on might have been ruined. Someone had senselessly damaged it without even considering her feelings or the work and care that had been put into building the booth. How could they do that? Didn't they understand how important this was to her?

When Marilyn got to Canada Place, she ran out of the car and hurried into the building. She went straight to her demolished booth and fell to her knees. A soft moan escaped her lips as she saw how the booth had been cut in half, and the signs had been ripped. Marilyn cried as she slowly picked up little scraps of paper and wood.

"Do you need any help?"

Marilyn stopped when she heard a voice calling to her. She saw a teenage boy standing beside her, hands in his pockets and head bowed.

"Pardon me?" she asked, still crying.

The blonde boy bent and started picking up paper too. "It looks like you could use some help."

Marilyn nodded softly. "Yes, this was my booth. It was vandalised tonight." She sighed and ran a hand through her hair. "We worked so hard on it for so long, and now it's ruined."

"I'm sorry," the boy said, his voice little more than a whisper. Startled, Marilyn looked into his large brown eyes. "We didn't mean to hurt anyone, honestly," he continued, "it was just for fun." The boy looked down, ashamed and embarrassed. He continued to pick up debris from the fallen booth.

After a few seconds, Marilyn placed her hand on the boy's shoulder. "Why are you helping me?" she asked quietly. "Why did you come back?"

The boy looked at her, tears in his eyes. "My mother was killed by a drunk driver two years ago."

"Oh, I'm so sorry. My son was killed by a drunk driver too. Actually, you kind of remind me of him. He was a good kid."

Marilyn wrapped her arms around the boy as his shoulders shook with the first sobs he'd allowed himself. Wind swept through the building and blew through Marilyn's hair while she sat, crying with the boy.

To Be Or Not To Be (Accepted)

Carli Pryce

My name is DaaL Skil. This means "rain that splashes on your face when you are on the water fishing." I am a member of the Haida nation. I am 16 years old. I have gone through a lot of tough times lately. People do not believe me when I tell them that. Well, I guess a person cannot believe anything unless they experience it themselves.

My family moved from my hometown. My hometown is a place that is very small and enclosed. There is not a place for teenagers to hang out, to have fun, as a normal teenager should. So all the teenagers from my hometown took different paths for life. We moved to a bigger place so that I could go to school. My parents moved because they were afraid that I would take the wrong path for life. They thought it would be best for me to go through schooling and get the education that I needed. I put a lot of thought into the talk that I had with them. I decided that maybe it would be best.

The day I went to school there was a lot of fuss. I had learned parts of the language required. English was very hard for me to learn. I had spent time watching TV and spent time around those who do speak it. I could not speak the language very well. I thought that my first day of school in my new area would go well. I arrived with a friend off of the reserve. We felt everyone gawking and staring at us. The two of us did not feel comfortable. During the day we had been talking to one another and a couple of other students overheard us. We were talking in our own language.

Later on that day we noticed that the students who had been listening to us were looking at us as we walked by and they were talking to the principal. We both figured that there was something kind of suspicious. Later on that day the principal approached me and said, " I understand you were speaking another language? May I ask what that language was?" he shook his head. "It would be unfair of you to speak another language in front of other students."

"Zum gum dung chu gun d'unshut ^gunga ut d^ goodimy stee gâ g^un g^shlow yêt shlow d lay shis goo la gun," I had said.

"Can you please translate that for me?" He had said to me with a confused look and angry sounding voice.

I told him I said "I find it very unfair that I can't speak your language very fluently. Why are white people able to speak their language amongst natives? The language is Haida Gwaii." He was not happy. I could tell this by the colour of his face.

The issue of me speaking the native language came to a point that parents of the students became involved. I was beginning to think that there is something wrong with the way I talk, the way I walk, and maybe even the way I think. I felt very uncomfortable. I felt like I was not good enough for these people that surrounded me. The principal decided that he wanted to hold a meeting with the trustees and board about the native language being spoken in class. The meeting created an issue amongst the community. People thought that it should be dealt with. After it was brought to the public's attention, it was said not to be allowed. This was how it was to be handled.

Their decision was brought to my attention and I disagreed with it so I wanted to fight against their judgement. I acted upon this, but I acted too much. My friend and I had been talking our language after we were told not to. We were spoken to again, but this time we were kicked out of school until we reached an agreement.

Everyday I was faced with fear. When I walked down the streets I got harassed. Everyone I walked by would name-call, not only to me but also to my family. They would put us down. I found this to be very inappropriate. All of the local people had heard about what the Haida natives were put through. There would be jokes cracked about our language or even our heritage. Some people would ask me "why were you created?"

My family said they could not handle what we were going through. "DaaL Skil I cannot handle this, but even if we do something about our conflict, I am afraid that it is not going to stop." That is what my mother had told me. She had tears coming to her eyes. I then felt very unhappy inside and out.

The next day my mom was feeling a lot better. She gathered up all of her strength from the previous incidents. She decided she was not going to put up with this anymore. She was determined that I was going back to school.

My mom decided to go and talk to my principal. She went to my school but deciding whether I was to go was hard. I then put on my shoes and ran out the door. I got there and I stood around waiting to see what was going to happen. I took a seat, and sat there patiently waiting.

My mom stepped out of the office. "So what happened?" I said to her, anxious to find out what she had to say.

"You mean what did not happen?" she said to me. "I don't think anything is going to progress out of this. He just ignored me." She seemed to me to be quite calm about it. I could not understand why of all people this had to happen to us. I thought back through time. It was all happening again. I understood the fact everyone was made the same on the inside and that there are people who do not understand that. It is hard to comprehend the way the world thinks about others.

My mother later told me that she did not appreciate being ignored. But she was not going to let it bother her. I could not stand to see my mother just ignore that fact. So I had to make a decision whether I was going to take action or whether I should just leave it.

"I want you to stay in school because you need your education. I didn't move here for you to do nothing and just sit at home like in our hometown. Do you understand? Your father and I have been talking about what happened and we do realise that it wasn't your fault. We would like you to stay in school for many reasons. You will be able to get a higher paying job than just making pennies." My mom was talking about my education. Sure, I understood, but because I was speaking a language that I can speak more easily than the other I got kicked out of school. That is the part not making too much sense to me. I wanted to go back to school, but I did not know what to do.

"I think that you should put some thought into why you should go back to school. It is worth going back because you can apply for a job that is a little more challenging. It would mean more money for you in the long run. After school we wanted you to apply to a college, maybe even a university. Education is very valuable to our family.

Your education can be useful in other ways too. You can use it to help others. For example, you could be a Native Resource Aid and go to the schools and help kids not to go through what you went through. You could be a Native counsellor and help either adults with problems or students with problems.

You get to create your own future. You would be able to pick what you want to do and not have to go by what someone says that you would be good at. You won't have to depend on others to do your thinking. You will have skills in demand. This is probably the most important one for your life. You'll have the ability to be what you want to be."

I could not think of a reason not to go back to school. I then thought of going to my boyfriend to get his opinion. I did a little thinking and then I walked over to his house. I talked to him about the whole thing that had happened in those past days and he got all heated up about it. He was not happy. He told me that I should act upon this but do a little thinking before I go right ahead. He was a great help.

"Well how should I go upon thinking about this?" I had asked him, anxious to see what he thought.

"It should be the traditional way of doing this. Maybe you could ask the chief if you could be put out on the water in the canoe." He said to me. I thought about it for a minute. I was kind of doubtful about whether it would be a good idea.

"I guess it could work. Let's go to the Chief to see what he thinks about this. I want you to think about this long and hard. Personally, I think that school is a waste of time. You should too; you have the name DaaL Skil, which means 'rain that splashes on your face when you are on the water fishing.' I think that you should be out on the water again. You need to be fishing with your family and mine. The traditional way is the only way in my point of view. Your family, traditions and heritage are very important to you, aren't they? Maybe instead of going to school you could just hang around me and take care of me so we could be happy together. Do women these days actually need the European schooling? In the past the native women didn't need it. They have had great lives for 100's of years now. And I am asking you, do you need it? Think of it this way, you could live free and hang out with all of your friends. But this is a decision that you have to make. Whether you listen to me or not it is completely up to you. It would be nice to see you more often than I do now. Don't you want that?"

We took off to see the Haida Chief to see if he thought that it was a good idea for me to do this. We got to his place and explained what the natives are being put through at the local school. He agreed that it was reasonable enough to go on the journey.

As soon as we got this news we went and told my friend. She was very happy about this news and she told me to have a good journey.

This journey was for me to learn about my life. I was to go out and clear my mind of all thoughts or to think of what to do with them. It was a chance to think about what I was going to do with the choices in life and to think about how to handle them. I never felt so excited in my life; I could already taste the salt water and feel the nice breeze.

It was a good time to think and a good way to survive. When I left, all the Band members were there to support me on my journey. I was happy that I was doing this. It felt good. It felt right.

I was on my way. I left and I was excited to be able to learn how to survive on the waters and be able to clear my mind about my conflicts and what had been going on. I was to learn how to survive on my own. I would learn how to fish and to purify the water from the salt.

On the second night while I was fishing for my dinner I spotted something. I looked into the water and I saw something I had never seen before. I saw images in my reflection that made me think about what I saw myself doing later on in life if I took one pathway and if I took the other. It was very serious and I just stared into the water. I thought for many a moment. All of a sudden a big pink salmon jumped into the canoe. After that incident I thought of myself as that salmon. I jumped for my thoughts about whether I should go to school or not. This fish was the open door to my thoughts and what I was going to do with them.

I saw a bird flying in the blue sky. The bird was so free, so utterly content by itself in the sky. It didn't have to go to school. It didn't have to worry about its culture. Its identity was secure. All the bird had to worry about was its next meal; otherwise it just had to float effortlessly on the wind currents, frolicking at will. It had no responsibilities. It had nowhere to go, nowhere to be. It was all alone. Tomorrow would be the same as yesterday and the next day.

After my long, extended days on the sea all that was going through my senses was the smell of the salt water. I was out there so long I felt like the water was the only thing that mattered. This all felt like I was there for a lifetime. I was beginning to feel very lonely. All I had for company out there was my dinner. The birds I hardly saw and the sound of the water splashing along the side of the boat coincided with my breathing. The water that was splashing on the side of the canoe kept splashing my face and finding my mouth. All that I could taste was the salt water and it was really getting to me. I could not handle the journey much more than I had to. This was the loneliest I have ever felt. I was beginning to realise I have everything made. All I was seeing was fish. I was very tired of these days; I did not want to be out on the sea with nobody around, no civilisation, only me. I needed to get home to my bed because sleeping on this hard surface was affecting my mind and my life.

These journeys usually last between three and seventeen days. I was very glad that I only had to spend three days out on the sea. To me it was a lifetime, a generation. The time I spent on the water forced me to reflect on myself and to address my very being. My spirit needed to be settled and satisfied. I needed to regain a healthy perspective. I was forced to look beyond my reflection and I did not like what I saw. I was on my way home and it occurred to me what I was going to do with my life. I decided that I was going to go back to school and just spend time with my boyfriend every chance I had.

Well my three days of traditional survival thinking were over and by this time I was focused and came back with greater understanding.

I thought about what I was going to do about my schooling. I came to the conclusion that I was going to deal with this myself. I wanted to go to the principal personally.

I went to the school to talk to the principal. I was thinking positively about what was going to happen. I learned how to be even more patient from my journey. So I waited around the school to see the principal. He came to his office ten minutes later to see what was going on. I had a talk with him. I knew I had to be rational and down to earth about the situation. I was very mellow about this. I explained the native history. I explained how I should not have to be assimilated into the European ways. The native language had been passed from generations. I should not have to drop my heritage all of a sudden because two non-native kids can't understand my private conversation.

I wanted to make specific, strong points that changed his feeling about how the natives should be treated. I wanted to put him in my shoes. I said to him "How would you, as a white person, feel about being put onto a plot of land with only your kind? You could not get an education unless you were assimilated into another culture. When you wanted to ride the bus, you had to wait for the bus with people of your kind. You would have to go to a native school, and you could only speak the Haida language and not English? Would you feel comfortable?" I said that to him with strength in my voice.

Slowly, and somewhat reluctantly, the principal agreed with me. I think it was the passion in my voice that made the difference. I was not angry. I was defeated. I told him about the way I had been harassed in the community and how alone and rejected I felt. He agreed to allow me back into the school, but I needed to ask my parents to go to the board to explain my position.

My parents attended the next board meeting. My only remaining concern was how I was going to be treated?

The day came for me to go back to school. When I got to the bus stop, none of my friends were there. I waited for the bus, but it did not show up. I ended up hitchhiking to school, and I arrived five minutes late.

My worst fears were realised. All the students were looking at me; I could feel their stares on my back. I reminded myself I was here for an education, not a popularity contest. I felt alienated in my own school, but I also felt trying to fit in meant I was ignoring my heritage.

I worked hard at school and began spending time with others in the school. We had many group projects that demanded time outside of school. My boyfriend and friends on the reserve stopped calling me. They stopped inviting me out. The people at school included me when there was work to do. I was very lonely. I was becoming what I had always fought against. I was being assimilated into the non-native ways and away from the heritage that my parents had taught me to know and to love.

One day we had to present a poem in our Language Arts class. I wanted to present one of the poems of my people but was not allowed to because they were not written and published. I searched hard for a poem that meant something to me. The books we had in school were about Shakespeare, Bacon, Wilde, and Swift. They did not share my world. Finally I found the poem that spoke to me. I presented Alootook Ipellie's poem, "Walking on Both Sides of an Invisible Border."

It is never easy
Walking with an invisible border
Separating my left and right foot

I feel like an illegitimate child
Forsaken by my parents
At least I can claim innocence
Since I did not ask to come
Into this world

Walking on both sides of this
Invisible border
Each and every day
And for the rest of my life
Is like having been
Sentenced to a torture chamber

Without having committed a crime

Understanding the history of humanity
I am not the least bit surprised
This is happening to me
A non-entity
During this population explosion
In a minuscule world

I did not ask to be born an Inuk
Nor did I ask to be forced
To learn an alien culture
With an alien language
But I lucked out on fate
Which I am unable to undo

I have resorted to fancy dancing
In order to survive each day
No wonder I have earned
The dubious reputation of being
The world's premier choreographer
Of distinctive dance steps
That allow me to avoid
Potential personal paranoia
On both sides of this invisible border

Sometimes this border becomes so wide
That I am unable to take another step
My feet being too far apart

When my crotch begins to tear apart
I am forced to invent
A brand new dance step
The premier choreographer
Saving the day once more

Destiny acted itself out
Deciding for me where I would come from
And what I would become

So I am left to fend for myself

Walking in two different worlds
Trying my best to make sense
Of two opposing cultures
Which are unable to integrate
Lest they swallow one another whole

Each and every day
Is a fighting day
A war of raw nerves
And to show for my efforts
I have a fair share of wins and losses

When will all this end
This senseless battle
Between my left and right foot

When will the invisible border
Cease to be

I saw something in the eyes of my teacher and classmates that surprised me. I saw, for the first time, recognition. Although they could not experience my life, they could view it. I realised that most people act out of ignorance, and I realised that I could help reduce this ignorance.

Everything happens for a reason no matter how painful. I know that being a Haida means I can be proud of who I am, and what I am about. I am proud to be a Haida human.

Un voyage inattendu

Andrea Jarman

Li-Lung est assise dans une petite chambre avec M. Ferguson, l'avocat qui représente les personnes du bateau, et son interprète. Pour la jeune fille de quinze ans, il est difficile de se concentrer sur ce qu'il dit.

Elle ne se sent pas dans sa peau depuis trois mois. Tant de choses impensables lui sont arrivées depuis ce jour au mois de juin dernier. Comment oublier? Ses pensées l'amènent en arrière.

J'étais victime de la rue en revenant du marché. Les odeurs m'attaquaient et me brûlaient la gorge. Les bruits me tombaient sur la tête avec force. La pollution me piquaient les yeux et m'aveuglait. L'air avait un goût âcre. Le monde était serré comme du bétail. Les autos klaxonnaient pendant que les marchands de la rue criaient pour vendre leurs marchandises. Je pouvais sentir le poisson pourri et ça me levait le coeur. Les gens me bousculaient en essayant de me dépasser. Je n'étais qu'une bulle d'air emprisonnée dans l'eau bouillante.

Quand j'ai finalement réussi à rentrer chez moi, mes parents m'ont rencontrée à la porte. J'ai su immédiatement que quelque chose n'allait pas. Le visage de ma mère avait perdu toute couleur et ses yeux étaient rouges comme si elle avait pleuré. Mon père m'a dit de venir prendre place sur une chaise dans la cuisine. Puis, il a annoncé la nouvelle qui me changerait la vie pour toujours... Nous avions été découverts. Le gouvernement chinois savait que ma mère était enceinte de son deuxième enfant.

J'ai couru à ma mère et l'ai embrassée. Je ne pouvais pas la lâcher. Je voulais être proche de son ventre qui tenait le frère ou la sœur tellement attendu. Mon père m'a dit de reprendre ma place. Il affichait un regard triste, il avait vieilli. C'était à ce moment qu'il m'a expliqué qu'ils m'envoyaient au Canada, ma vie était peut-être en danger et il ne voulait pas prendre de chance. On ne savait pas ce que le gouvernement était capable de faire de moi. Je voulais protester, les supplier de me laisser rester avec eux, mais j'ai gardé le silence.

Dans une semaine je devais partir, m'arracher de tout ce que je connaissais. Je devais abandonner ma famille, mes amis, ma vie. Même si j'avais entendu de belles choses sur le Canada, je ne voulais pas y aller. J'aurais tout sacrifié pour rester près de mes parents.

***

Pendant toute une semaine, je n'ai pas quitté mes parents. Ils allaient me manquer tellement, je ne voulais pas gaspiller cette derniere semaine que nous passerions ensemble. Je ne pourrais rien apporter pour me souvenir d'eux. Je voulais les calquer dans ma mémoire: leurs visages, leurs voix, leurs odeurs, leur amour.

Un matin, à leur insu, je les ai entendus parler. Entre les sanglots, ma mère implorait mon père de changer d'idée, de trouver une autre solution. Il n'offrait comme consolation qu'un rappel des dangers qui me guettaient si je restais ici.

Comment pouvait-il être si brusque, si vide d'émotions? Ne comprenait-il pas que je partais pour toujours? Il était évident que je ne valais rien à ses yeux. Je savais bien qu'il aurait toujours préféré un fils.

Quand je les ai vus sortir de leur chambre, j'avais l'estomac en noeud; les yeux de mon père étaient rouges et son visage était mouillé.

***

Nous nous approchions du bateau quand il est sorti du brouillard comme un fantôme. Il était vieux et rouillé et le peu de peinture qui lui restait était tout éraflé. Le nom Lily était écrit sur la proue mais c'était tout déteint.

J'étais entourée de gens qui n'étaient pas tous honnêtes et qui partaient pour le Canada pour des raisons différentes des miennes. Je voulais me cacher d'eux; ils me rappelaient les créatures qui se cachaient sous mon lit quand j'étais petite, ces monstres qui attendaient le moment parfait pour me saisir et m'amener dans leur monde de cauchemar.

Les démons, ces hommes qui avaient organisé ce voyage, me faisaient vraiment peur. Ils ont averti mes parents que s'ils ne recevaient pas le reste de l'argent deux mois après mon arrivée au Canada, ils allaient m'enlever. Je ne voulais même pas imaginer ce qu'ils me feraient s'ils me tenaient en otage.

***

Le premier jour je n'ai pas parlé. Je ne voulais pas faire partie de la foule affolée qui m'entourait. Puis une fille de mon âge m'a approché.

J'étais un bateau perdu, elle était un phare brillant. Une fois ensemble, rien ne pouvait nous séparer. Autrement, nous n'aurions jamais survécu. Elle était l'espoir, le soleil, le jour. Moi, j'étais le désespoir, l'obscurité, la nuit.

Les parents de Ai-Fu l'avaient envoyée au Canada pour qu'elle travaille et leur envoie de l'argent. Ils avaient toujours voulu un fils. J'ai peu parlé des raisons pour lesquelles je quittais la Chine. Je ne voulais pas qu'elle me dise que peut-être le Canada serait comme la Chine, que peut-être j'y serais aussi punie pour ce que mes parents ont fait.

***

Un jour malheureux restera imprimé dans ma mémoire. Ai-Fu était allée quêter de la nourriture, et dans son absence un homme s'est approché de moi. Au début, j'ai réussi à lui résister en me débattant, mais à bout de force je ne pouvais que pleurer. J'y ai laissé une partie de moi. J'ai dû succomber à ce bateau et à cette bataille que je livrais chaque jour avec une force invisible. Cette force qui faisait qu'il n'y avait pas assez à manger, cette force qui savait déjà le mauvais sort qui m'attendait au Canada. Cette force, je la détestais.

Je voulais courir, je voulais partir de ce bateau, je ne voulais jamais le revoir! J'étais prise dans un cauchemar et je ne pouvais pas me réveiller. J'ai crié, j'ai pleuré, mais ça n'aidait pas, j'étais coincée... condamnée à l'enfer. J'étais sur un bateau au milieu de l'Océan Pacifique avec ces hommes, qui n'étaient pas des hommes mais des monstres, des démons. Que pouvais-je faire?

À un certain point dans ma vie, avant ce voyage, je m'étais crue courageuse, persistante, que rien ne pouvait m'arrêter. Je voyais maintenant le tord que j'avais de me qualifier de même. Je n'avais pas de courage; chaque jour je voulais me cacher du monde, même me cacher de la vie. J'ai perdu la partie de moi qui était joyeuse. J'étais tout le temps sombre. Je me noyais dans mes larmes.

Il faisait toujours noir, noir partout. Même le jour, les personnes bloquaient le soleil et jetaient sur nous des ombres froides et peu amicales. Très souvent du brouillard épais comme une couverture nous couvrait. Cette brume donnait un air spectral à couper le souffle.

L'état du bateau s'empirait de jour en jour. Ça puait, il faisait froid, j'avais faim et je voulais rentrer à la maison. Je ne pouvais pas endurer tout cela. Ma tête était une bombe prête à exploser. Trop de sentiments, trop de haine. Des fois, quand je contemplais ce qui m'arrivait, je commençais à rire. Ça faisait peur à Ai-Fu. Elle me croyait sur le bord de la folie.

J'abhorrais ce bateau infernal, je détestais ces démons

abominables, mais ce que j'haïssais le plus? Attendre. Chaque heure me semblait un jour, chaque jour un an. Il n'y avait pas de fin en vue.

***

Le matin du 16 août, j'ai entendu un bruit aussi fort que le tonnerre. Le pont du bateau vibrait et une grande ombre passait par-dessus. C'était un avion.

Les démons nous ont crié de descendre au fond du bateau où c'était humide et froid. Il n'y avait pas d'espace pour bouger. Les mouvements du bateau ont rendu des gens malades; ça commencait à puer.

On chuchotait que nous avions été trouvés par les policiers canadiens et que nous allions être mis en prison. La panique m'envahissait. Est-ce qu'ils découvriraient ce que mes parents ont fait? Est-ce qu'ils me renverraient en Chine? Ça ne serait pas si mauvais s'ils m'envoyaient chez mes parents, mais s'ils m'envoyaient au gouvernement chinois, qu'est-ce qui m'arriverait? Et s'ils m'emprisonnaient, qui payerait les 65 000$ pour mon voyage? Mes parents ne pouvaient gagner autant d'argent en si peu de temps. Qu'est-ce que les démons leur feraient? Tout cela, pourrait-il être pire que ce que j'ai vécu?

***

Au débarquement, j'étais un bébé qui venait de naître. La terre fraîche me berçait comme une nouvelle mère et le soleil me souhaitait la bienvenue. Tout était nouveau, tout était magnifique. Je respirais pour la première fois l'air clair et léger, pas lourd comme à Nanguig, ma ville natale.

Pendant quelques minutes je ressentais le bonheur. J'ai réussi à oublier la damnation éternelle qui m'attendait ici, puis la réalité m'a frappée. Je voyais devant moi une vie de prostitution au Canada. Ce n'était pas la vie qui m'attendait, mais un internement insupportable.

Je m'accrochais à Ai-Fu. Je n'allais pas les laisser la séparer de moi. Nous étions les mailles d'une chaîne. Attachées et inséparables.

Quand nous sommes montés dans l'autobus, j'ai vu, dans la vitre à côté de moi, une fille. Son visage avait peu de couleur. Sa peau était gercée et pâteuse et ses cheveux noirs étaient gras à cause de la saleté. Elle était très mince, un vrai squelette. Je ne la reconaissais pas.

***

Je me suis trompée sur le Canada, ce n'était pas la prison infernale que je craignais. La vie a vraiment commencé à aller mieux après notre capture. Nous étions à Vancouver et pouvions faire ce que nous voulions. Dans quelques semaines, un tribunal déciderait si nous pouvions rester au Canada.

***

«Comprenez-vous? Est-ce que vous avez besoin que je vous explique une autre fois vos choix? répète l'interprète.

Choix, c'est la meilleure chose que j'ai entendu depuis longtemps. Mon voyage en enfer a pris fin. Le mot choix, c'est la lumière du paradis... Li-Liang respire profondément, puis répond:

- Oui, pouvez-vous m'expliquer une autre fois, s'il vous plait?»

Devon Buss

"I guess we zigged when we should have zagged."

— Submission Hold

Devon wrote "Le reflux du moment," the first story in the book. Devon is a grade 11, French Immersion student who was dragged into this project unwillingly but has thoroughly enjoyed the experience it has provided. In addition to writing for this book Devon had solo singing pieces in Highland's production of Pride and Prejudice this fall. Singing is a passion of Devon's and she plans to attend UVic and write music to be performed by herself and others. Devon lived her best experiences on Hornby Island and presently lives in the woods by the ocean. It is this setting that provided much of the inspiration for her story and has helped her develop her respect for all living beings.

Lindsay Chung

"A champion is someone who is bending over in exhaustion when no one else is looking."

— Anson Dorrance

Lindsay Chung wrote two stories, "The Hero," a story that tells of an elderly mariner pontificating about his adventures and "MADD About You," a story set in the 1980s of a mother who loses her son to drinking driving. This is Lindsay's second year writing for Highland's book and she is excited to be a part of this project again. She finds this a valuable experience as it helps her learn more about BC's history and improve her writing skills. Lindsay's researchers, Caleb Oppel, Chris Ptack, Jen Kolmatycki and Darcy Turenne (second book she has provided research for), were invaluable to her for her stories. Lindsay's writing has been compared to that of William Trevor, high praise indeed considering she has not read Mr. Trevor's works, yet. After graduation, she plans to go to university, study either English or Journalism, and ultimately pursue a career in writing.

Robyn Crouch

"The function of art is to do more than tell it like it is – it's to imagine what is Possible?"

-Bell Hooks

Ever since she was little, Robyn has greatly enjoyed art in all forms and has been consistently encouraged by her parents. She is definitely looking forward to continuing her studies of art at Highland, learning new techniques and perfecting old ones. Her art mentor has always been her dad. "He'll just walk by when I'm doodling or throwing paint on paper, and give me little hints about how I could make it better." Robyn prepared the picture on page 16 for "To Find a Raven in the Fog." Robyn plans to study at Emily Carr Art University in Vancouver.

Chelsea Eby

"Misunderstanding is my cornerstone. It's everyone's, come to think of it. Illusions mistaken for truth are the pavement under our feet. They are what we call civilisation."

— from The Poisonwood Bible by Barbara Kingsolver

Chelsea wrote "Caitlin's Promise," the story of an Irish-Canadian family in the 1960s. She has found the creative and collaborative processes valuable learning experiences. She enjoys reading and most of the authors she has enjoyed reading are women who have developed strong characters in their stories. Margaret Mitchell and L. M. Montgomery are the two that stand out in her mind. Chelsea is a passionate and nurturing person and that can be seen in her treatment of the protagonist in her story. Chelsea is grateful for the work her researchers Ann Scott and Kate Curtis did tracking down information for the story, and thankful for her Baba, Rose Leonard, for helpful insights from her personal experiences.

Destry Freeman

"Happiness is not a destination. Its a matod of life."
-Burton Hills

Visiting many art galleries in Paris (the Louvre, the Orsay, the Renoir, etc.) at the age of 12 with her mother and grandparents made Destry realize her appreciation for art and inspired her to further develop her skills in that area. Destry says she has been inspired by the sketches and drawing of Leonardo Davinci, but her "real inspiration comes from my parents and grandparents who also dray and paint." Destry learnt a lot of techniques and artistic skills from her grandmother. Aside from artistic pursuits Destry loves skiing, tennis, softball and playing the piano. Her achievements in any one of these areas are admirable. Destry prepared the picture on page 30 for the story "The Hero."

Julia Georlette

"Gravity cannot be held responsible for people falling in love."
-Anonymous

Julia was born in Antwerpen in Flanders during the spring of 1983. Following her dad sailing the oceans, she was exposed to many countries and cultures. The colourful Caribbeans remain close to her heart and further influence her artistic inclinations. She enjoys playing tennis, soccer and skiing. She has a vivid imagination, searching for perfection and the daily discovery of style and design allowing her sharpened skills to produce some critically acclaimed art work. Julia prepared the picture on page 112 for "Caitlin's Promise." Julia plans to pursue a career where her creativity would have the opportunity to flourish.

Gen Higgs

"Who do I want to be today?"

-Kevyn

Gen loves the prairies and is anxious to return. Gen is an accomplished synchronised swimmer and hopes to coach elite swimmers in the future. Despite her penchant for disorganisation and missed deadlines, Gen has a reputation for excellent work that provokes and provides thought. She likes to play and sing jazz music and plans to pursue this as a hobby. Despite her favourite colour being black, Gen is a very positive, up-beat person who tends to find the good in every situation. The process of writing for this book has forced Gen to stretch her limits and experiment with the medium. Gen is obsessed with shoes, however, it is her obsession with fish that can be seen in her story. Gen will likely major in kinesiology at a prairie university.

Sid Hughes

"Everywhere the human soul stands between a hemisphere of light and another of darkness; on the confines of two everlation hostile empires, Necessity and Free Will."

-Thomas Carlyle

Sid wrote "A White Man's Duty," an exploration of the moral dilemmas faced by many as they forged our province at a frighteningly fast pace. Sid enjoys sleeping, writing, sleeping, obsessing about things in his spare time, sleeping, disinformation, sleeping, knitting, and did we mention - sleeping. After graduation Sid plans to run a Yak ranch in a backwards third-world country or his back yard, whatever comes first. (Mr. Hughes notes that his request to the editor to have his biography set in larger and better-looking typeface was denied.) His dry wit and caustic sense of humour make him a pleasure and a misery to be with. Sid identifies Prozac as a key influence in his writing.

Andrea Jarman

"Never go to bed mad. Stay up and fight."

-Phyllis Diller

Andrea wrote "Un voyage inattendu," the second French piece in the book. Last year Andrea researched the history of Campbell River for Lindsay Chung and this year she provided her own research and wrote a publishable story. Other than her school work, there are two things that take up most of her time: sports and music. She enjoys playing and watching all sports but specialises in hockey and soccer. Andrea plays drums, trumpet and takes singing lessons and enjoys listening to most musical genres. Andrea enjoys watching others try and succeed in their efforts which gives her inspiration to tackle her own challenges. A French Immersion student, Andrea knows that the future is wide open to her and she is busy getting the most she can out of the present.

Mark Lewis

"The artist's first responsibility is to educate him or herself. Then try to pass along some information or direction to their audience."

-Little Steven

Ever since he was a small child, Mark has possessed a keen interest in the visual arts. Mark says that much of his inspiration comes form the works of fellow artists and he intends to continue developing his artistic skills through his entire life. He is a very academic-oriented student interested in a wide variety of topics; something which he says may have been affected by a habit of reading almost anything he can get his hands on. For Mark, the chance to create an illustration for this book and combine his interests in art, literature, and history was not to be missed. Mark prepared the picture on page 86 for "A White Man's Duty." Mark's plans for the future include attending university and finding a career where he can put his talents to good use.

Brennan Luchsinger

"All art is subversive."

-Pablo Picasso

Brennan is in his final year of high school. Born in Victoria, he grew up in Powell River and Comox. Brennan has many talents and enjoys many mediums of artistic expression. He enjoys the outdoors and finds great inspiration in the variety nature offers. Brennan's picture on page 42 of Vancouver's boat in Nootka Sound illustrates his interest in perspective. Brennan plans to spend next year at a local college preparing his portfolio looking for entry into an art school the year after.

Erika Manthey

"A believer is never disturbed because other persons do not yet see the fact which he sees"

- Unknown

Erika Marie Manthey wrote "Facing Change," a story of a family's struggles during the 1930s. Erika loves to write but is quick to point out that she is not the type of person who can just sit down and write for hours on end. She is inspired by nature and she values the lifestyle living in the Comox Valley affords. She considers herself blessed as she has been able to sample much of what BC has to offer from mountain biking, skiing, and swimming in the ocean, lakes and rivers, to horseback riding through unbroken trails on the country. Erika has not figured out what she really wants to do yet, but she is confident she will be able to achieve what she sets her mind to. Erika is grateful for the work Graham Latham and Robyn Bishop did in helping her research her story. Erika is a competitive volleyball player and is active in many facets of school life.

Katie Maximick

"If you love to do something you'll strive for it, but if you hate to do something, you want to get it over with."

— Katie Ann-Margaret Maximick

Katherine Ann-Margaret Maximick wrote "Journey of Survival," the story of a youth who is forced to grow-up quickly. Katie is immensely interested in writing and has already prepared a novel she is hoping to have published in the near future; she has also begun work on a second novel. Katie enjoys: drawing - she did the artwork for her own story - volleyball, music, singing, English, literature, and reading. Friends are extremely important to her. She is grateful for the work of Leah McGregor and Stacey McQueen in researching Fort Langley and the time period of her story. When asked why she writes, Katie's response is that "writing is like playing God, for you can invent whatever you wish, and the outcome of your characters' lives lay in the palm of your ink-stained hand." She adds that writing allows her to leave the stresses of the immediate life and escape to a world completely of her own creation.

Carli Pryce

"I know you think you understand what you thought I said but I am not sure you realize that what you heard is what I meant"

- Dawn Kozloski

Carli De-Ahne Alexis Janelle Clifton-Pryce was born in Comox, British Columbia. Carli spent her early years in Skidegate on Graham Island in the Queen Charlotte Islands, or as they are more appropriately named, Gwaii Haanas. Carli comes from a wide range of native ancestry. Her father is of Haida decent and her mother of Tsimshian and Haida decent. Her grand parents are of Haida, Kwawkiutl, and Coast Salish decent. From birth Carli has been very independent. This independence has helped her greatly as she has striven to achieve her many goals. She is very involved in the native community, dancing and sharing her heritage with others. Carli is an intelligent, kind, generous, and very caring young lady who is very respectful of her elders. She looks up to those who help lead her in the right direction.

Tyler Schwindt

"I am still learning"

-Michelangelo

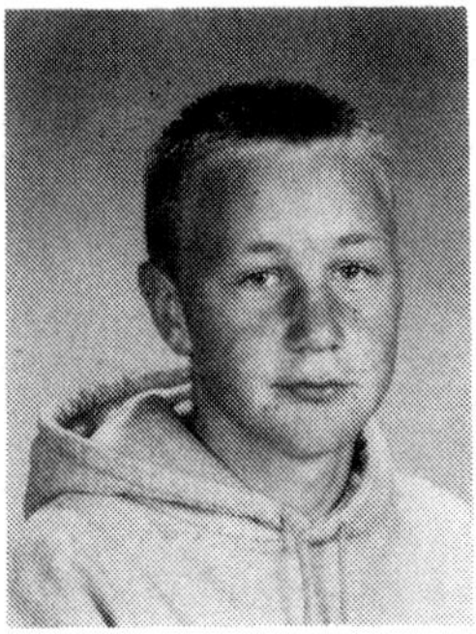

Tyler is a multi-talented individual who has many interests to fill his open mind. He enjoys snowboarding, skateboarding, playing guitar and drums. At school he enjoys English, Art and P.E. Tyler has worked hard to develop his artistic talants. His art teacher, Mr. Senner, has really helped to encourage him in his visual art skills. Tyler prepared the picture on page 91 for "A White Man's Duty." Tyler has not decided what he wants to do in the future; however, he is quite sure it will involve a musical career.

Chelsea Sinclare

"A conclusion is the place where you got tired thinking."

-Chelsea Sinclare

Chelsea has a flare for visual presenation. She is proficient in many artistic mediums and her work often evokes response. Art is her favourite form of relaxation and she uses it to express her thoughts and feelings. Chelsea has a knack for effective verbal communication and has a quick, incisive mind. Her picture on page 126 for the story "MADD About You" displays some of her ability to communicate through picture. After high school Chelsea plans to begin studying law.

Geoffrey Trotter

"The foolish man seeks happiness in the distance; the wise grows it under his feet."

-James Oppenheim

Geoffrey Trotter wrote "Nootka Nirvana," the story of a cabin boy on Vancouver's vessel who sheds the shackles of sterile, structured discipline for a night of enlightenment in Nootka Sound. Geoff is an award-winning stage writer and this is his first published prose piece. As an artist of both language and music, he takes great pleasure in the process of creating, in the forming of something unique and valuable where nothing existed before. Geoff thoroughly believes that there are many methods at an author's disposal to convey any particular idea, and that the search for the most effective of these methods is an absolutely critical element in writing. Geoff would like to thank Karli Durrant and Jason Vella for their research whose depth offered Geoff many possible directions in which to take the plot. Geoffrey returns annually to the setting of his piece for a summer camping trip, and hopes that some of the natural power which he experiences on a yearly basis will come through in his contribution to *Blazing Paddles*.

Allison Trumble

"Not all who wander are lost.

-J.R.R Tolkien

Allison wrote "Souvenirs," the story of a British socialite who arrives at Fort McLeod trying to avoid his pretentious past. She has greatly enjoyed working on Blazing Paddles, her first project of this magnitude, and has found it very rewarding. She often writes stories, poems and thoughts during her spare time, and finds it a great release from the pressures of life. Allison enjoys photography and develops her own prints in the darkroom. She is also an accomplished athlete starting on the Senior Field Hockey team in her Junior year. For the future she plans to study language and literature at the post-secondary level. After that, she will do whatever interests her.

Megan Turner

"Imagination is more important than knowledge."

-Albert Einstein

Megan was born in Gander, Newfoundland. She loves to draw and sketch in her spare time, especially cartoons and animals. Most of her ideas come from bits and pieces of images that she has seen either in ads, on TV, or on book covers. When she is not in school or doing homework, Megan can be found practising in the pool with the Comox Valley Sharks competitive swim team, or on the court playing basketball. Megan prepared the picture on page 55 for the story "Nootka Nirvana". After she graduates in a year and half, Megan plans to work towards her Masters degree in either Marine Biology or English Literature.

Ruth Viers

"Art is reaching out into the ugliness of the world for vagrant beauty and the imprisoning of it in a tangible dream."

- George Jean Nathan

When asked what she is happiest doing, the immediate reply is, "Intent on drawing." Art has always been a focal point in Ruth's life, and she hopes it will continue to be. Author and poet Edgar Allan Poe has been a great inspiration to Ruth. His openness to the darker side of writing has given her new perspectives. When asked to draw for *Blazing Paddles* she immediately jumped at the chance and challenge of capturing the story's romance. Ruth drew the picture on page 58 for the story "Souvenirs." In the future Ruth hopes to develop her skills and create something memorable.

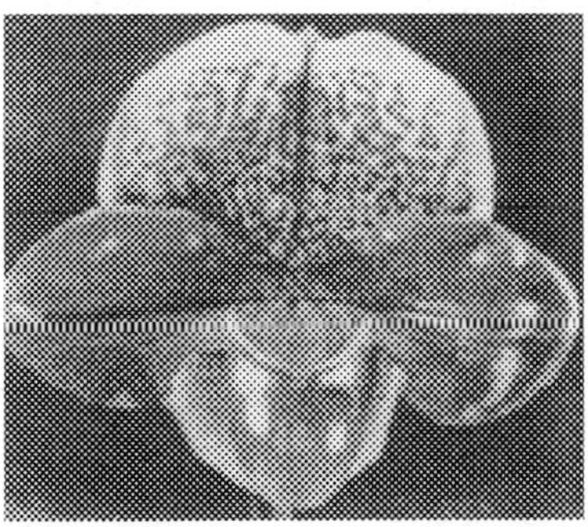

Afterward

This is the third book in an increasingly popular and professional series.

In October 1997, a group of students in Summerland got together to discuss BC history only to realise that there was very little interest in the subject. There were two reasons identified that explained the largesse: 1. the history written was not accessible to the students due to the inflated style of writing and 2. the common perception that history was boring. These students decided that instead of lamenting the fact, they should do something about it. The result was a week long trip to the coast where they researched their topics at the BC Archives, Ross Bay Cemetery, Helmcken House, Point Ellice House, The Union Club, Royal British Columbian Museum, Maritime Museum, Native Information Centre in Duncan, and through personal interviews. The result was *We Are British Columbia: Essays of Interpretation.* The book received considerable recognition from the academic community as well as from people with general interest. The students achieved their goal of making it accessible and the book is being used in classrooms for Social Studies nine and ten.

> The students have uncovered plenty of fascinating details about a wide variety of British Columbians and different places in the province. It is interesting to view BC history through the eyes of young people and see what information caught their attention. There are fourteen articles on Aboriginal peoples, land claims, the Queen Charlotte Islands, education, and major and minor figures (both men and women) in our history.
>
> *We Are British Columbia* is a tribute to the energy and enthusiasm of the students involved in its production. Considering the age of the students and the short timeline under which they operated, it is an impressive example of a high school history project. In his recent book, *Who Killed Canadian History?* historian Jack Granatstein lamented the failure of our schools and

> universities to properly teach Canadian history. A reading of this student-produced book would likely give him hope for the future.
>
> *BC Studies, 121, Spring 1999*

All aspects of the book were completed at the school except the physical printing. The book involved 14 students from start to finish. *We Are British Columbia: Essays of Interpretation* was profitable in two weeks and the skills the students learned will never be forgotten. Several of the essays have been favourably used to augment existing curriculum resources and have also been cited in academic work via the Internet.

In October 1998, a group of students at a different school had a similar epiphany. Instead of purely addressing the accessibility issue, the students decided to show how entertaining British Columbia's history can be. The resulting book, *Stories of Our British Columbia*, has received exposure in Europe, Australia, the Eastern United States and Canada, as well as throughout British Columbia. The book contains six short stories chronicling BC's past. The stories are historically accurate in setting and the events are legitimate; however, the plots are fictional as are the characters. This book involved over 70 students from conception to profitability. The book was profitable after being on the market 13 days.

> Congratulations, on behalf of the Ministry of Aboriginal Affairs, to all of those students whose vision and hard work has created such a marvellous collection of stories. All of these students should be extremely proud. For youth to capture part of British Columbia's history on paper, and to tell each story creatively through art and words that both respect and display our diverse culture, will help to capture the past and inspire the future.
>
> Gordon F.D. Wilson,
> Minister of Aboriginal Affairs

> Forget about being written by students, there are some excellent stories in this book. This was an ambitious project, and the results are well worth the effort.
>
> Toby Lustig, *Comox Valley Echo*, May 21, 1999

> **Highland students 'making history.'** But even more than some fascinating B.C. history and terrific creative writing, the project also tells the story of co-operation and hard work by those involved.
>
> Jennifer Blyth, *Comox Valley Record*, May 28, 1999

> As diverse as the students who wrote them, the stories in this book are passionate, insightful, entertaining, and a must read for anyone living in or interested in British Columbia. Well written and researched, these stories allow the reader to vicariously visit the mind that is British Columbia.
>
> Donald Banks, *The Beacon,* May 1999

> The reality is that the students had a dream. They worked tirelessly to achieve their dream, on their own time, as the club is not part of the curriculum. They were focussed and professional in their efforts and the overall quality of the book is spectacular.
>
> Barry Wood, *Comox Valley Record*, June 1999

> Critics agree the book is very inventive, well written and assembled and is a "must buy."
>
> *North Island Weekender*, June 18, 1999

Stories from Highland's last book are used in English classes and Social Studies classes with great success. Students appreciate the quality and the accessibility of the stories and enjoy reading them. The stories are entertaining while being informative and are not written for an audience of limited abilities. The illustrations have received rave reviews and commendations. The book has also provided tourists with a reasonable sampling of BC's past as well as an appreciation for the quality of education provided students in our province. Two of the authors graduated last year and are attending post secondary schools while the others remain active in the school. All have commented vociferously of the value of the experience and the benefits it provided them. Several have been contacted by publishers to provide their writing skills.

Stories of Our British Columbia was so successful that Highland Secondary School was encouraged to produce another book of British Columbia's history. Anytime a project encourages large numbers of students to show an interest in their heritage and the culture of their province, it provides immeasurable value. World-renowned author of Canadian history, Pierre Berton, has written the Introduction for *Blazing_Paddles: Historical Fiction of British Columbia* citing the importance of such projects and the skill with which it has been dispatched. Local published authors such as Matt Hughes, Des Kennedy, Nelson McInnis, and Jeanette Taylor have worked with the students on this book.

Afterward

What began as a group of frustrated youth has developed into a project of true quality and value. In reading these stories one must forget that they are written by students and focus on the writing, it is excellent. Each story offers its reader an experience designed to portray the essence of the era in which it is set. After such reading, your comments are encouraged and invited. The writers want feedback on their stories: positive and constructive.

Are you wishing you had bought your own copy of *Blazing Paddles* or perhaps that you had bought more than one copy?

Could you use more copies for:

- A gift to friends? A gift to relatives from another place?
- A souvenir of your holiday in BC?
- Showing your Social Studies class that "history" and "interesting" are not mutually exclusive terms?
- Showing your school board, English and Humanities departments, or parent advisory council an example of the amazing things that youth can accomplish if given the support and opportunity?
- Use in an English class as examples of great short stories?

Copies are $15.00 each.
Class sets of thirty books cost $375.00.

Alternately, purchasing a license to the text of the book for use *within a school setting for educational purposes* which includes a compact disk containing the text of the stories to format, print, and distribute to your students as you desire (with no limit on the copies you can make) costs $200.

For availability and order information, see the *Blazing Paddles* web site at:
http://sd71.bc.ca/highland/blazingpaddles

Or phone Highland Secondary School at (250) 339-5525.